D1569175

Freedom in White Mittens

Raelene Phillips

Cover Illustration by Ed French

This book is lovingly dedicated to
Vondale and Floyd Wood,
my Mom and Dad.
They taught me to always do my best.
("Why isn't this B in English an A?")
They also made me believe that with God's help I could
do anything I really wanted to, even write a book!
I love you both—ReRe

ACKNOWLEDGMENTS

This, my first book, could never have been written without the help of some people very dear to me whom I would like to acknowledge.

First, my sister-in-law, Tammy Wood. She has developed as a hobby a serious study of geneology. At the time of this writing, she has traced both of my parent's blood lines back hundreds of years and compiled all the facts into notebooks. Among the facts, I found the story of a rich boy from Germany who ran away to America with his poor girlfriend. They were separated and sold as indentured servants. A pair of mittens played an important part in their story also. At my mom's urging, my imagination took over and *Freedom in White Mittens* was born. Thanks for the idea, Tammy.

Next, three very special people—my husband, Danny; our 16-year-old daughter, Sonya; and our 14-year-old son, Kyer. They have put up with "quickie" meals when I spent all day with a notebook and pen in hand. I'm sure they lost sleep when I'd get an idea in the middle of the night, and the typewriter's clicking seemed deafening. But they never complained. They have listened patiently as I read entire chapters aloud and asked for their opinion. Invariably they said, "It's good, Mom!" or "I like it, honey!" They've encouraged me every step of the way. Thanks, you guys—I love you!

And, of course, Eleanor. Though separated by miles, her interest in this project never failed. Phone calls, cards, and notes of encouragement always came when I needed them most. For this I named a character for you—in chapter 20. Thanks for being my B.F.

Raelene Phillips
Philippians 4:13

Part 1

Beginnings

Chapter 1

he sun was just beginning to break through the morning mists as Hannah opened the cottage door. A stiff wind tossed her brown curls into her eyes before she got the fascinator tied over her hair.

"Aach! Aunt Hilda is right! It *is* cold enough to freeze the man in the moon!" Hannah grumbled as she pulled on old brown work gloves. If she didn't get the rest of the garden truck harvested today, a hard killing frost would take it tonight for sure. She would have to wrap the new tomatoes in brown paper and place them in the cellar. They wouldn't taste as good as if they had ripened naturally on the vine, but it was better than allowing them to go to waste. She knew she could leave the carrots in the ground, but that was not her goal.

At the memory of her goal, Hannah smiled. Aunt Hilda often made fun of her for her goal setting. "Whyn't you just do whatever the good Lord places before you to do each day 'stead of always trying to set goals on yourself, girl? Seems all you accomplish is setting yourself up for a big letdown ere you don't make your daily goals!"

Hannah tried to explain that it gave her a sense of accomplishment to try to make her daily goals. Aunt Hilda was married and had already raised her family. 'Twas little she knew of the fruitless feeling a young orphan like Hannah often felt. Knowing that no one in the world cared much about you made a person have to care more about herself—or else die of loneliness!

"And so Aunt Hilda, on the days when I don't make my goals, I just put them at the top of the list for the next day. It gives a sense of rhyme and reason to my life. And I need that!"

Thus their arguments always ended, and Aunt Hilda would walk away shaking her head, realizing that she would never understand this child of her brother. Hannah had come to live with Peter and her after the terrible accident five years ago last fall.

"So today I will get it *all* harvested!" Hannah mumbled to herself as she climbed over the slight rise to the garden plot. She paused for a moment. 'Twas a beautiful morn, in spite of the cold that seemed to increase each day as the summer catapulted itself into autumn. The sky was bluer than the back of the jay chattering in the huge oak near the garden. The leaves of the maples were still green, but Hannah knew that 'ere long they would be all crimson and gold. Down yonder at the far end of the field, the lofty pines marched in formation, their deep blue-green standing out against the sky. Breathing the crisp clear air that almost hurt her lungs, Hannah scolded herself as she trudged into the garden. "No time for foolish daydreamin'," she grumbled. "Carrots, potatoes, tomatoes, squash, pumpkin—they will all be in the cellar ere I drop on my cot this night."

Hannah never even thought of harboring any ill will because all the work was falling on her. Peter Junior could certainly have helped, for he was a strong lad of 13 years and nearly as tall as herself. But he was ever his mother's favorite, and she always found excuses to keep him from any form of labor. Gertrude, at age 14, was busy at the loom today, and heaven forbid that anyone suggest that Katrina soil her hands in the garden. With her wedding only a fortnight away, Katrina spent endless hours embroidering all the linens for her dowry chest.

Thus the outdoor work fell upon Hannah. She did not mind because she loved to be outdoors. Even the cold wind whipping her shawl at every step was a welcome relief to the stifling atmosphere of Uncle Peter and Aunt Hilda's home. Their home was really little more than a hovel. Built of rough logs which had not been finished in any manner inside or out, the house was actually just one large room. It had three windows, but none of them had glass in them. Instead they were covered with a greasy papyrus-like paper which admitted only a minimal amount of light, that being a sickening shade of orange. In the room were crowded all the daily necessities of the six people who lived there. Uncle Peter and Aunt Hilda's bed and dresser were in one corner. The north wall was nearly all fireplace. Placed before it were two straight chairs and a big bulky quilt frame. A loom and spinning wheel were shoved against the far wall. A rough, hand-hewn table with long benches on each side stood near the door, and a corner cupboard was shoved behind the door. Right square in the center of the room was a ladder which led to the loft where the children slept. The house was always extremely hot and stuffy and smelled of lye soap, for Aunt Hilda was convinced that cleanliness was next to godliness.

So Hannah was always glad to be out in the fresh air.

Oh, she was grateful to them for taking her in when she had nowhere to go—but would Aunt Hilda never stop reminding her of the magnitude of their sacrifice on her behalf?

All these thoughts tumbled in Hannah's mind as she bent over the row of stubborn carrots. The wind had placed two rosy spots on her otherwise pale cheeks. And the blue in her eyes was flashing as she remembered how again this morning Aunt Hilda had remarked on the amount of food consumed by "the extra person at this table."

"Mayhap they don't want to be pulled yet, my lady!" said a deep voice a few yards to her right.

Hannah had been so deep in thought as she tugged on the carrot tops that she hadn't heard the approaching horse's hoofs. She jumped so quickly that the toe of her clumsy ill-fitting shoe caught in her skirt and she nearly fell headlong. Her innate grace saved her from falling, but she was genuinely flustered when she looked up into the eyes that belonged to the deep voice—none other than William, the son of the Lord of Stivers' Castle!

"I don't believe we've had the fortune of meeting before, My Lady. My name is William. Would you care to tell me yours?" he asked.

Can this be happening to me? Hannah thought. Aloud she said with a deep curtsy, "Oh sir, you are mistaken! I am no lady. I am only the orphan servant girl who lives yonder in the cottage owned by Your Grace."

"Do you have a name?" he asked once again, this time a trifle impatiently.

"Begging My Lord's pardon, my name is Hannah Duffy. But I cannot imagine why one such as yourself would want to know!" Immediately she knew she had made a dreadful blunder. She did not want Sir William to think she was being smart with him. But her tongue now seemed glued to the roof of her mouth. Her eyes filled with tears as her face and neck grew scarlet.

"Don't grow flustered, My Lady," said he as he swung down from the saddle. "I know of the great divergence in our backgrounds. And I hate the social ethics that demand that because of the difference in our stations in life we can never become friends. You see, I have watched you as you work in the fields here as I run errands for my father. Please do not think me bold, Miss Duffy. I am not trifling with you. But I thought ere I left my room this morning, 'If I do not make her acquaintance today, I shall go mad!' "

Hannah could not believe her ears! She had often seen him galloping by on the great black stallion. He had always doffed his hat to her. In fact, sometimes at night she had allowed herself to fantasize about Sir William. But this was no fantasy! He stood there! His black eyes bore into her own. Then a shadow crossed her mind—perhaps he thought because she was a mere servant he could have his way with her. Her eyes snapped! "Sir William, I know I am a poor girl but I am also one of high moral Christian character! I . . ."

Now it was his turn to blush as he interrupted her. "Oh please, Miss Duffy—hear me out. I know I've bungled this badly. But my intentions are totally honorable. I would have approached your uncle openly. But we both know that no one in this land of ours would understand the son of a Lord wishing to become . . . uh . . . friends with an orphan servant girl! Would that we were in a different place and time where I could just be William Stivers and you Miss Hannah Duffy and we could walk in the moonlight together and get to know one another."

Hannah stood speechless before him. Could it be true that he was interested in her? At a glance she had noted every detail of his appearance. His hair was jet black as were his eyes, and he must be just beginning to grow a beard and moustache, for his face was outlined with a soft-looking black stubble. But the new beard did not hide a square jawline and a dimple which was just a little off center in his chin. He was just one head taller than Hannah, so as they talked she needed to tip her head slightly back to be able to stare into his beautiful black eyes. He emitted an aura of quiet strength from his wide shoulders down to his trim waist. For some reason Hannah noticed that his hands seemed extremely large, perhaps because he nervously toyed with a jeweled riding crop as he spoke. He was dressed in the finest wool; a tweed jacket topped his riding pants. Even his boots of fine kid seemed to scream out, "I belong to a rich man!"

By comparison Hannah thought herself to be a humble waif. She did not know that what William was seeing was the long brown hair which blew in wispy curls around her face, and eyes the color of the sky in summer. Her nose was perfectly shaped and led to a rosebud mouth. Her simple, drab dress gave no clues except where it was obviously too small across the top and Hannah's lovely young figure strained at every seam. All of her clothing seemed to be brown and ugly. But the girl herself was quietly beautiful.

"Isn't there any way we can . . . uh . . . become friends?" he pleaded.

Though a bit fearful of the consequences, Hannah could see now that Sir William Stivers was indeed sincere in his desire to befriend her. She dropped back to her knees between the garden rows. Did her complete shock and utter confusion show in her face, she wondered. Toying with the carrot tops, she spoke as if to the ground.

"Oh sir, I cannot see a way. Thank God in heaven this garden grows over the rise from Aunt Hilda's cottage for I know that were she to see us talking I would be punished. I thank you for your kindness in noticing me, but I don't

7

know if we should . . ." Her voice trailed off as she sat back on her heels and stared upward again into his eyes.

"Would to God this were America!" he nearly shouted, for his feelings ran so deeply.

"Ah—America!" She nodded. By now everyone had heard of this brave new land where men were said to be free in every way.

"The freedom in America is not just religious in nature," said Sir William, now in a more controlled tone of voice. He stared off toward the western horizon as he spoke. "In America, if a man does not want to do what his parents expect of him, he does not have to do it! If he likes to plow around in the earth and grow things, he is never told that the job is beneath him. And he is free to choose for himself the girl he wishes to marry!"

Hannah sat shyly before the eloquence of Sir William's speech. She had never heard a man go on and on like this. The men of her acquaintance had all been painfully silent individuals.

"Do you like to farm then, Sir William?" she asked cautiously.

"Like it?" He grinned the most infectious smile she'd ever seen. He knelt beside her and picked up a handful of the rich loam. "I love it! I never feel so close to my God as when I am digging in the earth, planting seeds, watching the miracle of growth, and harvesting the bounty that grows. I long to plant acres and acres—but, Mother will only allow me a small garden plot as a hobby." Now the sarcastic tone returned. "For, after all, we are the *landed gentry.*" He emphasized these last words with utter and complete scorn. "We rent out cottages to serfs and they do the work of the estate. We sit and get fat and die of boredom!"

Hannah had never imagined in her wildest fantasy that Sir William would share her love of the earth. "Would you care to help me pull my carrots?" she ventured.

"Oh, Miss Duffy, could I?" He spoke with the eagerness of a child.

So they worked side by side that morning, talking of life. As the sun rose higher in the sky, Hannah removed her shawl. Sir William took off his tweed jacket, and Hannah wondered how his mother would react when she saw the dirt on his fine silk shirt. But of course there would be maids to care for the washing in Stivers' Castle.

She had never dreamed there could be one like him who seemed to share her every thought. He even commented on it. "We are as alike as two peas in a pod, Miss Hannah."

Neither was sure when he had dropped her surname in their chat. It had just happened naturally.

"Hannah!" came a shrill shout from the cottage.

"Oh dear! Look where the sun is. I should have heated up the soup for their lunch an hour ago," Hannah exclaimed as she grabbed for her shawl.

"And I must go into the village," Sir William said dejectedly. "Oh Miss Hannah, may I see you again? Please?"

He took hold of her elbow to help her to her feet. The touch of his hand sent a thrilling shock through her whole body.

"I don't know," she mumbled. It hurt so much to leave this morning behind. She couldn't remember ever having felt so totally alive. "How can we . . ." she began, but broke off shyly.

"Tonight. After all are asleep and the moon is full. Meet me here in the garden. Please," he implored.

"Hannah! Where are you?" shouted her aunt.

"I'm coming," Hannah screamed. "Oh dear, I don't know if I can or if I should . . ." she barely whispered.

"I'll be here!" he stated matter of factly as he picked up the bags of carrots and potatoes they had dug and handed them to her, his hands resting ever so lightly on her own. "I'll try," she called as she ran over the hill to the cottage.

Chapter 2

ould this day never end! As usual, Aunt Hilda had changed Hannah's plans for her, thereby making it impossible for Hannah to complete the goals she had set for that day.

"The rest of the garden truck will just have to wait till tomorrow," her aunt had insisted. "I doubt there will be a hard frost anyway. And I want you to wash all the bedding this afternoon."

Once again Hannah was grateful for a job which took her outdoors. But, oh, what a tiresome job it was! First she must build the fire just so under the huge washing kettle, then shave the cake of lye soap into the water and stir till it began to boil. Of course, the back-breaking work was scrubbing all the sheets on the washboard. But as she did all of this and then hung the sheets on the line, her mind was in a whirl, vacillating between her options.

For a moment she thought perhaps she should try to forget Sir William even existed. Then she knew she desperately wanted to meet him tonight. Then her mind would tell her it was futile. All that a friendship with Lord Stivers' son could ever bring her was grief. But oh—her

11

heart! She kept remembering the thrill of his touch, the joy of his laughter, and the shine of his eyes.

Over and over in her mind she kept remembering one sentence he had uttered when he spoke of that distant land of America. "And he is free to choose for himself the girl *he* wishes to marry!" Could she dare to hope? No, it was too impossible for words.

All through dinner Hannah tried to keep her mind on the table conversation. Uncle Peter spoke of having hauled grain to the market in town today. "Lord Stivers should be pleased. The men at the mill told me it is a seller's market this year. His two-thirds share of the profit amounts to almost half again over what we paid him last year."

Aunt Hilda and Katrina spent most of the meal discussing what kind of stitching she should use on her linens. Since Hannah had never been taught the fine art of embroidery this topic held no interest for her either.

Peter Junior and Gertrude were arguing as usual, until Peter Junior noticed Hannah's lassitude.

"What's the matter with Hannah? She hasn't eaten a thing. She's just picking at her food. If I didn't know better I'd think *she* was the lovesick one getting married in two weeks instead of Katrina," he taunted.

Now the whole family stared at her, and Hannah could feel herself blushing.

Aunt Hilda grouched, "Is something hurting you, child? Lands, I hope she isn't going to come down sick. Katrina and I will need her help desperately these next weeks."

It was so infuriating the way they all talked about her as if she weren't there. But Hannah always tried to treat them kindly, remembering all they had done for her.

"No Aunt, I am not sick. I do have an awful aching in my head though."

Uncle Peter looked concerned. "Mayhap the child should go to bed. She may be coming down with the ague."

12

"That's a good idea, dear," Aunt Hilda responded. "Just as soon as you have done all the dishes and tidied the kitchen, go to bed, Hannah."

Later, as Hannah dropped on her cot, she thanked God once again for her own room. Though it was totally free of adornment and ugly beyond belief, at least it was hers. The floor slanted precariously toward the rear of the house, and the wide bare floor boards were rough on the soles of her feet. There was a box which had originally been a crate for Aunt's dishes in the far corner of the room. It now held Hannah's meager belongings, except for the woolen dress which hung on a wooden peg by the door. Hannah's uncle had built a shelf above her low cot upon her request, only to be berated by Aunt Hilda for "spoiling that child beyond belief." Hannah tried to keep something pretty on her shelf at all times. Sometimes it was just a bunch of wildflowers. Sometimes a dead butterfly. Often just some pretty stones.

This was the one place in the cabin that almost seemed like home to her, this sad little afterthought of a room. It was the one concession her aunt and uncle had made on her behalf. Though the other three children all slept in the loft of the cabin, they had allowed Hannah to inhabit the lean-to porch at the rear of the main room. Hannah suspected that it was allowed so that she could arise early and cook breakfast without disturbing her cousins. But no matter, tonight she was especially thankful that she could close the door on the rest of the household. More important, she could also leave the house via the porch door without disturbing anyone.

As Hannah lay on her cot waiting on the rest of the house to quiet down for the night, she went over every detail of her morning hours spent with Sir William. At first they had talked only of the garden, sharing with each other their own special tips for growing the biggest and best vegetables. But then Sir William had begun to share with her the frustrations he felt as a member of the landed gentry of Germany. His elder brother would inherit Stivers' Castle and all the land someday. Yet, William was required to do all the "expected" things—preside at special dinner parties, collect the rent from the cottages, go on fox hunts (which he hated), and so forth. Hannah remembered the fervor in his voice as he spoke of America. She also remembered his infectious laugh when she mimicked her Aunt Hilda. Never had she felt so at ease with anyone.

A tap at her door interrupted her reverie, and as it opened, she could just make out her aunt's silhouette in the waning light of dusk. "We're going to bed for the night," she whispered. "Are you feeling better, Hannah?"

"Yes, Aunt—I was almost asleep," she fibbed. "Good night."

"Good night, Hannah. I hope you are fully recovered tomorrow. There is much to do."

As Hannah lay in the darkness, she prayed it was not a sin to go and meet her new friend. *Aunt and Uncle have never actually told me not to go out at night so it is not an act of disobedience*, she reasoned with God. She tiptoed to the peg on the wall and took down her old woolen dress, slipping it over the one she had worn all day. She knew it was even uglier than the first dress, but one must be practical. It would be cold out tonight! She pulled on an extra pair of stockings, then very cautiously opened her bedroom door.

Standing as still as a statue she could hear Uncle Peter's snoring. She peered through the darkness toward their bed in the opposite corner wondering if Aunt Hilda was asleep yet. Hannah did not know how long she stood thus before the moon broke through the clouds. A moonbeam fell across her aunt and uncle's bed just as her aunt's arm dropped over the edge. Since she did not pull her arm back under the covers, Hannah was sure she was asleep. Cautiously closing the door, she tiptoed over to the outside door, and passed noiselessly through it.

Oh, please, don't let me get caught! she prayed as she ran to the garden. The moon shone brightly on the frost, turning the countryside into a fairyland of light. She slowed after she went over the rise and her heart dropped; Sir William was not there. Just then, however, a form jumped down from the huge oak tree. Hannah started in fright.

"Did I scare you, My Lady?" he chuckled.

"Oh, at first I was scared that you weren't here. I thought perhaps this morning had been a dream."

"A good dream, I hope," said he with such hope in his voice that she couldn't help smiling.

"Oh yes, Sir William. The best dream I've ever had. I never knew that having a friend to talk to could be so exciting."

"I trust your aunt was not too upset over her dinner being delayed this noon," he said.

"Oh no—I was not in any trouble if that is what you mean. But this afternoon she made me wash all the bedding so I could not meet my daily goal. She knows that is a very effective way to punish me."

"Not meet your daily goal? I fear I do not understand."

Hannah giggled. "Most people do not understand. You see, I spend a few minutes each morning setting goals for myself to accomplish that day. It seems to give a reason for my existence. I suppose it is a silly habit."

"Not silly at all," he interrupted. "A very admirable quality, I would say, especially in one so young. How old are you, Miss Hannah?"

"Not quite seventeen years, sir." She shivered as she spoke.

"Oh—you are cold. Here add my cape to your shawl. Shall we walk? The air *is* a bit nippy."

And so they set out down the path on foot; a path on which he had ridden his horse that morning. When he reached for her, it seemed so natural that his arm would lie protectively across her shoulders, helping to hold the cape in place.

As they walked, Sir William drew out of Hannah bit by bit the story of her life. He learned of the awful day five years earlier when she had watched the sailboat in which her parents were joy riding capsize on Lake Martin. Even now the telling brought tears to Hannah's eyes. "But kind sir, I have told you all about myself. What of you? I know naught of your life."

They had come to a small stream which was lined with trees. Without speaking of it they sat down together on a log near the water. The trees sheltered them from the wind and Hannah finally stopped shivering as Sir William spoke.

"Well, I am just three years your elder, having been born in the year of our Lord, 1732. Perhaps I should hasten to say that the most important thing in my life is my faith in the Lord Jesus Christ."

Hannah couldn't help gasping. "Oh, Sir William, it is another thing we have in common then. I am a Christian also."

Sir William seemed awestruck. "I hadn't even dared to hope that you would be in agreement with my beliefs," he whispered.

He grasped her hand in the silence. Her confession of faith seemed to give him new urgency and concern.

"Miss Hannah, the time grows short. See how the moon has traveled across the sky. We must return to our homes ere we are missed. But I must share with you what is in my heart before we go back. I told you this morning that I have admired you from afar for a long time. Now that we have met and talked, I know of a certainty that it was

16

meant for us to be together." Hannah's mouth dropped wide open and she stared unbelievingly into his face.

"I can see by the shock in your eyes that this is all happening too fast for you. Would that it could go slower so you could get used to the whole idea. But My Lady, I must leave this land. In two days hence, I leave for America!"

Hannah gasped. A cold fear clutched her heart. Now that she had begun to get acquainted with Sir William, how could she go on without his friendship?

He continued as he rose and began to pace in front of her, "Miss Hannah, try to understand what I am about to say. My parents arranged a marriage for me years ago. The wedding is to take place one week from tomorrow. She is a baroness. The mixing of the two fortunes, you see. But alas, my lady, I do not love her. In fact, I loathe the woman! And I *will not* marry her. So, cowardly though it may seem, I have chosen to run away."

Hannah finally found her voice. With bowed head she quietly said, "I do not think you cowardly. I think it is very brave to leave all you have behind. But are you certain you must?" She tried not to whine, but knew she was doing a poor job of hiding the longing in her voice.

"Yes, Miss Hannah, it is the only path for me. But let me hasten to speak on before I lose my courage. I know it is too soon to speak of these things, My Lady. I know we have not had a proper acquaintance and all of those things, but Miss Hannah I want you to come with me to America."

Hannah raised her head in wonderment. What had he said?

"I know it is a surprise, and I'm sorry. But, Miss Hannah, I want you to be my wife. We would have to leave secretly tomorrow in the night. Could you . . . would you . . . ?" he stuttered.

Hannah's eyes filled with tears. As she looked up at him, they spilled down her cheeks and sparkled in the moonlight.

"I'm sorry. I didn't mean to upset you. I only hoped . . ." he muttered as he stood, turning away from her.

"Shh," she whispered and quietly walked to his side. "Sir William, these are not sadness tears. They are for the joy in my heart. I shall never understand why one such as you would choose me, but I would be honored to be your wife. And I will go with you anywhere."

They stood thus in the moonlight, each entranced by the other, their fingers entwined like two school children. Neither spoke; the moment seemed holy to both of them.

Finally, William broke the silence. "Much as I hate to go, we must, My Lady. You have made me happier than I had ever hoped to be."

As they walked back to the garden plot, they made plans to meet the next morning in the garden again, out of sight of the cottage. This would seem perfectly normal to Aunt Hilda as to finish the harvesting would be Hannah's first goal for tomorrow since she did not complete it today. William would make all the necessary arrangements and they would finalize their plans tomorrow.

When they got to the rise in the land, William took back his cape. He took Hannah's chin in his hand and whispered, "Thank you, My Lady. I will see you in the morning." Then he turned and was off across the field like a rabbit.

Hannah hurried to the house, for the cold penetrated her every fiber. As she stole into bed she whispered aloud, "He never even kissed me." But a grin played at the corners of her mouth as she fell asleep.

Chapter 3

t was hard to pretend that to-day was just an ordinary day when Hannah knew that by tomorrow at this time she would be Mrs. William Stivers. But she must contain her happiness; already as Hannah stirred the corncakes for breakfast the cold scrutiny of Aunt Hilda's eyes penetrated her.

"My, my! For a girl who took to her bed with the chickens last eve claiming to have an awful aching in the head, you certainly are pert this day, Hannah."

"Ah yes, praise be!" Hannah replied. "The aching left me in the night and today I feel right as rain. Old Bossy gave her milk this morn without grumbling for a change. So I finished the barn choring early. Shall I call the cousins to breakfast, Aunt?" she thankfully changed the subject.

Hannah kept telling herself to hold the joy in check lest anyone suspect what was to come about this day. She hummed as she cleared the table and washed the dishes. Inside she was all aflutter, but on the outside she appeared calm.

"This is my wedding day," she sang to herself as she emptied the dirty, sudsy water out behind the cottage.

"And a more beautiful day I've never seen." Truly the fall air was sharp and crisply clean. The sky was so very blue and the trees were a riot of color. Of course it would be tonight—perhaps way into the night—before she and William would be wed. She wondered if he had been able to locate a justice of the peace nearby.

Still trying to maintain the charade of normalcy, Hannah spoke to her aunt as she bundled herself against the cold.

"Well, today I simply must get all the vegetables into the cellar else we shall lose half of them. I shall try, how-ever, to watch the sun closer today and return on time to fix dinner. See you at noon."

"Yes, yes—be gone with you, Katrina and I need all the floor space to lay out these quilt squares. Child, I still don't see why we can't use the plain nine-square pattern instead of that new one. We only have ten days or so to piece and quilt . . ."

As Hannah pulled the door shut on the argument she felt a twinge of jealousy. If only the accident had never happened, her mother might be helping her piece a quilt— a quilt that Mr. and Mrs. William Stivers could sleep under! But then, had it not been for the accident, more than likely she never would have met Sir William.

God doth truly work in strange ways sometimes, she thought. For the first time ever, she could see some good in the tragedy of five years ago. That queer twist of fate had placed her here on Uncle Peter's farm, a farm owned by Lord Stivers who sent his son, Sir William, to collect rents. That's how yesterday's meeting in the garden had been ordered by the Lord.

With her thoughts going around inside her head, Hannah tried to keep herself from running to the garden. In case any of her relations were looking out a window, she must remain calm.

Once over the rise, however, her feet fairly flew, carrying her straight into the arms of the waiting William. He embraced her tightly and their lips met, first shyly—then with such intensity that finally Hannah pulled away from him!

"Good morning, my darling!" she panted.

"Where have you been?" he asked. "I've been waiting at least an hour. I was beginning to think that in the cold clear light of day you might have changed your mind. Oh Hannah, you haven't—have you? You will come with me tonight, won't you?"

She smiled at the boyish pleading in his voice. "Yes, just tell me when and where to meet you and I shall be there." He sighed in such relief that her heart was touched.

"Could we meet here again? I shall tie Midnight down near the creek so no one will hear us leaving. Can you come earlier tonight?"

"Not without risking detection," she answered. "Now I must be at my work of harvesting. Talk to me as I work, or I shall not complete the task again today."

"I'll help you," said he and began to break the zucchini from the vines. "Come as early as you can, My Lady. For I want to put as many miles as possible between myself and the castle ere morning breaks."

"I'll try," she promised. "But Aunt and Uncle are not often early to retire for the night. And I feel I must be sure they are asleep or they might hear me leave. Will you wait for me?" she pleaded.

"Of course, Miss Hannah. I would wait forever if necessary."

They laughed often as he laid out his plan to her. They would head straight across Germany into Holland. He estimated it would take a month to get to Amsterdam if they had to walk every step of the way. But as soon as they were far enough away from Stivers' Castle, they could catch rides on the road. Tonight, however, they could not travel on a road. They would head cross-country through the fields.

Suddenly Hannah became confused. "A moment, Sir William," she interrupted. "If you are going to tie Midnight near the creek tonight, why will we need to walk or catch rides? Why won't we ride on him?"

William sighed. "Would that we could take him along! But he is part of my plan. I shall tell Mother tonight that I yearn for a ride in the moonlight. She will protest of the dangers as she always does. Then I shall simply never return from that ride. We will ride Midnight about two miles from the castle. Then, after we dismount, I shall slap him with the riding crop; he won't stop till he gets to the horse barn. I'm hoping everyone will be convinced that I met with some mishap in the dark, for there he will be all in a lather with my saddle still on."

"But they will search for you," Hannah protested.

"They will not search as far from home as we will go. Sooner or later someone will decide that I am dead," he laughed.

"I hate all this deceit," said Hannah as she dragged the sack of squash to the edge of the garden.

"I know, My Lady. I hate it too. But I can see no other way." He changed the subject. "Will you have much baggage? We can only carry the bare necessities."

Now it was Hannah's turn to laugh. "Sir William, I will not have *any* baggage. I had on everything in this world that I own last night, except a locket Daddy gave to Mama once. That is my only keepsake. But you will have much to carry, I presume."

"No, Miss Hannah," he retorted. "I am determined not to take any of my possessions from the castle, for you see, none of it is truly mine. It all belongs to me only because of the family connections, and I feel I must break all those ties. I want to make it in the new world truly on my own, not relying on the wealth of the castle to support me." He laughed heartily. "We shall be a wonderful pair with only the clothes on our backs to call our own!"

Hannah kept waiting for him to complete the plans. When and where would they get married? But he talked about other things. Finally, she could stand it no longer.

She began shyly, "I can hardly believe that tomorrow by this time I will be your wife. But where are we to be wed and by whom?"

William sat back on his heels in the dirt. His mouth hung open. "What did you say?" he asked.

"You said you would make all the arrangements. When and where and by whom will we be wed?" she repeated.

"Oh, My Lady—I—I thought you understood," he began weakly. "I asked you to come with me to America and to be my wife, in that order. I did not mean for us to marry until we reached America."

Hannah stared at him incredulously. She tried to pretend that the instant tears in her eyes were from the onions she was pulling so diligently. But Sir William was not fooled. "I'm sorry, my dear. I don't see any way but the one in my mind. If we were to marry near here it would be too easy to trace our identities. And I want us to use our real names when we are wed. As we've already said, there is too much deceit. Can you see that it would be better to wait?" he implored.

Hannah was confused. "But, Sir William, how can we travel together and not be wed? It isn't right. How would we—uh—care for our daily needs?" She felt herself blushing, but felt she might as well continue. "How would we sleep?"

Now he blushed also. "Miss Hannah, I will never compromise your virtue if that is what your are asking. I thought mayhap we could pass ourselves off as brother and sister."

"I understand the need for secrecy hereabouts," she reasoned. "But why can we not marry when we get to Holland?"

He had hoped she would not ask that question. He feared her response to what he must tell her next, but tell he must. There must be openness and honesty between them.

The harvesting was completed now with a few minutes to spare before the noon mealtime. He gently took her hand and walked over to the oak tree.

"Miss Hannah," he began quietly. "There is another reason we must wait to wed. I will take no money from Stivers' Castle tonight. I will not be guilty of thievery."

"So?" she asked. Her big blue eyes stared intently into his.

"So we will not be able to earn enough along the way to pay for our passage to America once we get to Amsterdam."

"How can we go then?" the confused girl asked.

"We can sell ourselves," said he.

At the look of horror that crossed her face he hurried on. "Now, do not panic. I have heard from my uncle, the sea-faring Stivers' brother, that this is done all the time. The ships will allow strong able-bodied young people to cross the ocean on the condition that when they reach America some wealthy person may buy their services for a certain length of time. They are called indentured servants. The land owner pays the ship's captain for them."

Hannah was visibly crushed. The tears that filled her eyes threatened to spill over before she wiped them away, leaving a dirty smudge across both cheeks. Her hands trembled within Sir William's large ones. She longed to throw herself against the tree he leaned on and sob out her despair. *Is my beautiful dream life to end before it begins*, she wondered. "How long must one be a slave?" she whispered.

"Not a slave—a servant, my little one. Uncle Henry said

24

the time varies from about three to six years. But most often a master gets four years of servitude for the payment of the crossing."

With an idea, Hannah brightened. "Mayhap some rich American would buy a strong looking married couple?"

"Oh, Miss Hannah," he cried. "I wish that were true. But we cannot be certain. And I do not think I could bear it if we were separated once we are married."

"I shall not be able to bear it whether we are married or not," she cried. "So let us go ahead and wed and pray to God that He not let anyone separate us when we go into this—servitude."

He couldn't help but be relieved that she had agreed to the route of indentured servanthood he had chosen as the only way possible for them to get to America. How could he help her understand the rest?

He could feel his face coloring as he began to speak of the indelicate problem. "Miss Hannah, I love you and I want you to be my wife with all my being. But we simply must wait until we are free in America. If we were to wed tonight or even in Holland, where would be the guarantee that you would not be—uh—in the family way ere we ever arrived in America?"

Her eyes flashed confusion, then silent peace. At last she understood. She was embarrassed that she had been so thick-headed. Of course his plan was the only sensible one. But could they pass for brother and sister? How could she wait months—no, years—to become his wife!

Involuntarily, she glanced at the sky. The sun was straight overhead.

"Oh, Sir William, I must go," she exclaimed. "I am so muddled in my brain that I cannot even think. I know not whether I can do all you ask of me."

He raised her hand to his lips. There were tears in his eyes. "Mayhap it is too much to ask. If so, I beg your for-

25

giveness, and my God's. I only know that I love you, Hannah. I will wait here until the moon rises halfway between the horizon and midsky tonight. Please, *please* come to me."

With that he bounded toward Midnight and was off without a backward glance.

Hannah wearily toted all the bags of vegetables to the house, her head in a spin. She washed her face in the icy water at the well before entering the cottage.

"It's about time! I thought I would have to yell for you again! What's gotten into you, Hannah?" grumbled Aunt Hilda.

Chapter 4

ears dripped off Hannah's chin that afternoon as she worked in the cellar. She stacked all the squash on the third shelf beside the pumpkins for future use.

How could a day which began so beautifully and full of promise have turned so dismal? she thought. *Was it only this morning that I was daydreaming about being married?*

The day had darkened along with Hannah's mood. There was a real chill in the air, and a strong wind blew dark clouds eastward.

The bittersweet ecstasy of being kissed by Sir William crossed her mind with restless longing. "Why did it ever have to begin if it had to end so soon?" she whispered.

But did it indeed have to end here? Why was she so afraid of the fantastic adventure Sir William had outlined to her? It always came back to the same thing—"I wouldn't be afraid if we could just be married!"—yet she knew that Sir William was being sensible. They could never face the hazards ahead of them should a child come their way.

"But what are my alternatives?" Hannah wondered

aloud. The sound of her own voice echoed in the small root cellar and Hannah had to smile. "Aunt Hilda would think I'd gone mad for sure were she to hear me talking to myself!"

Hannah was removing all the lacy green tops from the carrots, saving some of the tops for the evening soup. She carefully laid the carrots in the sand table which Uncle Peter had built solely for preserving them. Filling the bottom with carrots, being certain they were never touching lest they spoil, she then shook sand over that first layer of carrots and started the process over. If Aunt Hilda was careful there should be plenty of carrots to get the family through the winter. The layers of sand would preserve them so they could have fresh-tasting carrots all winter long. As she did all this the possibilities ahead of her rushed to and fro in her confused mind.

"If I don't go with Sir William tonight, I shall probably live the rest of my life here in Uncle Peter's house." Hannah knew that the girls in town already referred to her as "Peter Junior's old maid cousin." Most of them had married by the age of thirteen or so.

Well, and would it be so bad to live here forever? she wondered. But before she ever completed the thought, Hannah felt a wave of repulsive anger. *If only Aunt Hilda did not treat me as a slave!*

Her thoughts now jumped ahead to what would become of her in America if she joined Sir William tonight. *There I would not only be treated as a slave, I would* be *a slave!* No, what was that word he had used? Some kind of a servant. But no matter, it still amounted to being little better than a slave. The only difference was that in America it would last for a few years—and then she would marry Sir William. If she stayed here her servitude to Hilda and Peter was all she could expect to ever do with her life!

When she looked at it in this light, the decision became so easy! And so finally, after hours of soul-searching as she worked in the cellar, Hannah determined in her heart that she would join her lover in the garden tonight! She would simply put all these fears out of her mind and trust God to lead their steps. She remembered part of a Bible verse Papa had taught her years ago from the book of Isaiah. It said, "Thine ears shall hear a word behind thee, saying, This is the way, walk ye in it." She hoped she was not guilty of taking that verse out of context as she applied the words to her present situation.

"Lord," she said as she dropped her head, "I truly believe that my meeting with Sir William was not by chance or accident. He loves You as I do. Though I know not why, I believe he loves me, too. So, I thank You for him. And I pray that in the years to come we will always hear Your voice behind us telling the way we should walk. Thank You." Hannah rested quietly for a few moments in the sweetest peace she had felt in years.

The carrots were finally finished. In fact, all of the vegetables were now in their proper place, and Hannah was glad to have completed this goal.

As she opened the cellar door, a cold rain struck her face, and she was soaked by the time she reached the barn. After milking Bossy, she threw a fork of hay down for the team of oxen, then ran for the house.

"Aach! Don't be dripping all over the house, Hannah," her aunt screamed. "Peter, you turn your back. Hannah, you step out of your dress right there and run to your room to put your other one on." As Hannah did her aunt's bidding, she shivered with cold. She grabbed a rough towel and dried her long hair hastily, then brushed it out in front of the fire near where her aunt had hung her dress.

"Aunt Hilda, a bit of time remains before I need begin

supper. The sorting and storing of the garden truck went quickly. Would it be all right if I looked into your mirror to braid my hair?"

Before her aunt could protest, Katrina interjected, "Let me do it for you, Hannah. My eyes are tired of the embroidery work, and your hair is so fun to work with. It is so thick and nice. It does whatever I bid it."

And so it was for one brief interval that afternoon Hannah felt like a bride, being served by others. She asked Katrina to braid it very tightly, then wind the braids around her head. Little did Katrina know that she was helping Hannah prepare for her flight tonight. If her hair were tight to her head, it would be much easier to run through a dense forest. No twigs would catch at the long curls to slow them down.

Somehow Hannah endured the last supper in her aunt and uncle's house although time seemed to almost stand still for her. She made extra corn bread, for two purposes. First, her relatives could at least have corn bread and milk without her here to cook for them on the morrow. Then, too, she hid some of it under her shawl on the shelf in the bedroom. It would get Sir William and her through tomorrow without starving.

She thought for the second night running that the family would never decide to go to bed. Aunt Hilda burned the lamp much longer than usual to finish piecing the first section of Katrina's quilt. At last Uncle Peter complained that the lamp oil was low, and they all retired.

Instead of undressing, Hannah dressed for the night. She put on all her undergarments one atop the other. She also slipped her locket over her head. Then came the cotton dress, the wool one, her shawl and fascinator.

Thankfully, Aunt and Uncle were very tired this night and fell asleep almost instantly. Being extra careful, Hannah carried her shoes out the door. When she was about twenty feet from the door, she sat on a stump to put them on.

As she glanced back at the house, not a pang of remorse took hold. "It pains me to speak so," she whispered, "but I shall not miss any of you. I do pray God to keep you safe, but as none of you ever gave me any love, I shall not have any call ever to long for my home. My home will be with Sir William."

With that she was off and running over the rise, into the arms of her future husband. He hugged her briefly, then hurried her toward the stream and the horse.

"Speed is of the utmost urgency," he panted. "We must be as far away as possible ere dawn breaks."

What an exhilaration she felt as she clung to him on Midnight's back! The horse ran like the wind over the fields; she felt her tight squeeze of William was justified. *It simply wouldn't do to fall off.* She smiled at the thought.

All too soon she felt the animal's pace slowing. "This is it," said Sir William, as he helped her down. Immediately, he whacked Midnight hard on the rump with his crop. "Get on home," he shouted as the horse galloped off. With a smile on his face he made an elaborate scene out of dropping the silver headed crop on the road.

"Now, My Lady, you must drop the 'Sir' from my name. And I'd like it if you would also not call me William. For Sir William Stivers of Stivers' Castle, Germany, just died. Henceforth, I shall be Will Stivers of America! Agreed?"

She couldn't help catching his enthusiasm. "By all means, Will—now what?" she teased.

"Follow me," he said after a quick kiss on the cheek. "We must hurry!"

Hannah never knew how she made it through that night. He led her through deep woods, over hills, and through steep-sided ravines. With only the moonlight to guide them, he never seemed to waver at all as to which direction to go. Most of the night he was fifteen to twenty feet ahead of her. Only once did their endless trek stop. Hannah had slid down the last ten feet of a steep trail on the seat of her dress trying to catch up to Will.

"I—I'm thirsty," she coughed as she landed at his feet.

"Oh, My Lady, I'm sorry. I knew not that you weren't right behind me. We will rest for a while yonder by the stream."

Hannah chided herself for slowing their progress. But when she drew the corn bread out from under the shawl, William seemed so pleased that she did not stay distraught for long.

"Oh, Hannah, it tastes so good. I have been so nervous these last two days, I have hardly eaten at all."

After they had each drunk their fill from the clear stream water, they started west again. This time William took her hand and she did a fair job of keeping apace with him. Just as she was convinced she could not move another step, he stopped.

"Look behind us, Hannah. Isn't it beautiful?"

They had just come to the top of a hill. As she turned around, she was entranced by the most beautiful sunrise she could ever remember.

"Oh, Sir Will—I mean Will,—it is as if God has painted the sky so vividly just to shower His blessings on the beginning of our lives together."

She felt his arm slip around her waist. She did not realize that her body was trembling with weariness.

"Sit you down, My Lady. If you look east you can watch the sun rise. If you look west it is still dark and the moon is nearing the horizon. You rest while I build you a sleeping place."

"No, Will, we must go on," she protested weakly. But he explained that he had never intended to travel by daylight till they were farther away from the castle.

"There is a heavily-wooded glen just over the rise. We

shall rest there today out of sight of any who might pass."

Hannah was almost asleep sitting straight up when he returned a few minutes later. He half-carried, half-pushed her deeper and deeper into a bower of pine trees. He had scooped up the fallen needles into two big piles about an arm's length apart.

"Now you sleep well, my little Hannah," said he as he laid her on the first pile of needles.

"You are so kind to me," she mumbled with her eyes closed as he kissed her on the cheek. "It feels so good to lie down."

Sir William gently lay his own cloak over her before he laid himself down on the other bed of pine needles. It did feel good to relax!

"Goodnight, Will—I love you!"

He sat bolt upright. Did she even realize that she had never said those three special words to him before? He smiled, but he could not answer, for she was fast asleep.

Chapter 5

he sun shone brightly all that day, but the bower of trees protected Will and Hannah from its rays. The trees grew so thickly that hardly a speck of light penetrated. The traveling pair slept the sleep of the dead, totally exhausted.

For a moment, Hannah could not figure out where she was as she sat rubbing the sleep from her eyes. When she tried to stand, every muscle in her young body cried out for relief.

"Where on earth am I and how did I get here?" she muttered aloud as she swept the pine needles from her dress.

"So, you finally awoke!" someone said.

As she turned toward the voice it all came back to her. There sat Sir William Stivers cross-legged before a small fire on the other side of a trio of trees.

"What is that delicious aroma?" she asked as she joined him.

"I trust My Lady fancies roast rabbit. I fear we may grow tired of it ere our journey is complete," he apologized, as he pulled the crude spit out of the fire.

"Oh Will, I find that I am ravenous. Here, in my pocket, I saved us each a bit of corn bread."

"A feast fit for a king!" he joked. "But, shall we pause to thank the King of Kings for our feast?"

As they bowed their heads, Hannah thanked God silently for a truly spiritual head of their future home.

"How did you manage to catch this rabbit when you carry no weapon? And how long have you been awake while you let me sleep? I fear that I am holding you up on your journey to freedom. You shall surely wish ere long that you'd left this clumsy girl behind." The girl said all of this without pausing for breath. Will was beginning to see that Hannah was not always shy.

"One question at a time," he responded. "And no more of the silly talk about not wanting you along. You shall simply help me to pace myself. I oft have a tendency to overdo physically and thus exhaust myself. Now, let's see—as to the rabbit, I used this slingshot. And I haven't been awake all that long myself. You were so sweet when you awoke just now."

"I often have the problem of not being able to figure out where I am when first I awake," she said, lowering her eyes. "Sometimes it scares me out of my wits. The rabbit is delicious, Will. How did a rich boy ever become so adept with a slingshot?" she teased.

"The groom which Father hired when I was a wee lad taught me how to shoot out back of the stables. I went through a time at about age ten when I shot at birds for sport. I never dreamed the talent would ever be useful to me," he chuckled.

"It's getting dark," she noticed. "Shouldn't we move on?"

"It looks darker here amid the trees than it is. But yes, we may as well begin again if you feel up to it," he replied as he helped her to her feet.

"I feel wonderfully rested and quite full. If only there

were something to drink," she wished aloud.

"Your wish is my command," he laughed as he pulled her through the bower to a babbling brook.

They headed straight for the setting sun after Will had kicked dirt onto the fire. He had kicked their pine needle beds all over the area also, to destroy any trace of their camp.

"Is that necessary?" she asked as they trekked along.

"Can't be too careful," said he. "In case they search farther from the castle than I presume they will, we must be careful of our campsites for another day or so."

Each of the travelers wondered aloud what their respective families were thinking and doing about their disappearance as they walked. But soon the terrain became rough again and it took all their energies just to stay afoot. The sun disappeared all too soon and it grew dark almost instantly.

A few hours had passed until Hannah began to fear that if she had to continue to follow Will through this wilderness in the darkness she would lose her sanity. So she began to do as her mama had often bid her as a tiny child.

"Hannah," she would always say, "when you are fearful or lonely, just sing."

Will was surprised to hear her lovely contralto voice as she carefully plodded along behind him. She sang old ballads, love songs, and some hymns.

Will was just about to blend his own tenor voice along with her on one of the hymns he recognized when suddenly he heard hoofbeats.

It all happened so fast. Hannah never could remember exactly what had transpired. All Will could think of was that Hannah must stop her singing, lest the rider of the horse detect them. Instinct told him he dare not risk calling back to her to be quiet, else his own voice might give them away. So he leapt quickly back to her side and, clamping his hand over her mouth, he pushed her over the side of an embankment. Will grabbed the trunk of a young tree with his left arm, never moving his right hand from Hannah's mouth. He felt hot tears fall onto that hand but before he could explain his rough treatment to his lady love, two horsemen galloped past not five feet from where Will's left arm clung to the tree.

As the hoofbeats died away, Will loosened his hold on Hannah. Only then did he realize what a large steep hill they were on, for she began to slide away from him.

"Will—help me!" she whispered. There was no moon, and Will could not see her. Her moans came up to him from straight below.

He pulled himself back up to level ground and talked to her soothingly. "My darling, I'm so sorry. Are you injured? I did not mean to treat you so brutally. But I heard the hoofbeats, and we dared not be seen yet. Hannah, where are you? Are you hurt?"

"I'm down here," she sobbed. "It is all rock and I am cut and scratched. My left hand hurts so bad. I feel every beat of my heart in it."

"I will climb down to you," he said as he dropped his legs down over the cliff.

"No!" she said in a half-whisper. "It is too steep and dangerous. I fear you will fall. But Will, I must know. Were the riders from the castle?"

"It was so dark—can't be sure. But I fear they must have been. I thought I recognized my older brother's voice, but it may not have been him. I was so busy wondering what you must think of my awful treatment of you that my mind was in a muddle."

She tried to laugh. "Do not berate yourself. I am all right. And you had to silence my singing! If only my hand didn't hurt so, I would try to climb back up to you and we could be on our way. Perhaps if I—"

"No!" he interrupted. "Stay where you are. For we have no way of knowing how steep this ravine is, and I cannot risk having you fall deeper. If only I had not loosened my hold on you! Hannah, is there any way you can make yourself comfortable until daylight? It must be only a few hours off."

"Oh, Will, I am so tired I think I could stand straight up and sleep. But again, I am a burden to you. We should—"

"No, Hannah! You stay where you are! This accident has taught me an awful lesson. We will no longer travel by night. It is too great a risk. My lady, let us try to sleep till dawn. Then we shall get our bearings and go on."

"Thank you, Lord," Hannah sighed. But before she fell asleep her hand bothered her so that she moaned. "Oh Will, my hand throbs!"

"Place it above your heart, dear. The less blood reaches it, the less it will swell. I shall pray for you."

Will slept fitfully. He kept waking in the middle of a dream where Hannah fell down out of his sight. The horses' hoofs and her sobbing mingled time and again to make him jump in fear, only to realize he was dreaming.

Hannah also had a rough night. In her case it was not her dreams, but pain which kept her awake.

Finally, as the light of day broke over the edge of a large hill, Hannah began to emerge from the deepest sleep of the night. Will was at her side wiping her face with wet strips of smooth cloth.

"Oh, my lady, what have I done to you?" he moaned.

"What? Why are you bathing my face?" Hannah mumbled, not yet fully awake. But then she stared at her hand in horror.

"It must be broken," Will sighed. Her hand was nearly three times its normal size. It had turned every shade of purple and black overnight.

"Your shirt!" Hannah gasped as she realized that Will was wiping blood stains off her face with wet strips of silk.

"Yes, I found a stream out in the middle of this meadow before you awoke. It is wondrous cold. Do you think you could . . ."

But before Will had completed the sentence Hannah had struggled to her feet. "Where?" she asked.

Together they stumbled to the edge of the water. Hannah fell to her knees, then dropped her face into the water. When she had drunk her fill, she sat up and held her throbbing hand in the icy water.

"It feels good," she said as she looked around. They were in the middle of a large meadow. Grasses grew nearly waist deep. But for the birds in the air and the large fish she could see in this clear stream, she and Will might be the only two living creatures on earth.

Will had removed his shoes and was wading into the stream. After several false tries he gleefully held a big fish in the air. They were so plentiful he had caught it with his bare hands.

Later, sitting by the remains of a fire and picking over the bones of the delicious fish, Hannah sighed. "My hand does not ache as much since you had me tie it up in this sling. "But, Will, I feel so dirty. Would that I could bathe myself." She couldn't believe she spoke so boldly without blushing.

"I was thinking the same thing," said he. "This stream is so clear. Let us find a proper way."

And so it was that he tied both their cloaks in the trees' branches, making a wall of privacy for their bathroom. He also helped Hannah to unbraid her long hair. When he handed her a ball of scented lye soap, Hannah's joy knew no end.

"Did you think of everything?" she asked incredulously.

"I tried," he replied. "Now, My Lady, whilst you enjoy

39

your bath I want to go back up the little embankment where you fell. It is quite a ways off, but there is something I must check. Will you be all right?"

She appreciated his concern for her privacy. She stepped behind the "wall" of cloaks and slipped out of her clothing. The sunshine was bright enough to warm her skin, but the mountain stream was like ice water! After the shock of the initial plunge into the water, it felt good. She swam a few yards. It felt so good to be unencumbered of the tight clothing. But remembering why she was in the water, she soon was making a lather with the soap. It was awkward to wash the long curls with just one hand, but she managed. Then as Will had still not returned, she took the liberty of scrubbing some of her underthings and the two dresses. She had just wrapped herself in his cloak and was spreading her clothes on a bush to dry when he returned.

"Oh, Will—I feel so much better! I see some berries yonder among the trees. Why'nt I go pick us some while you clean up? I left the ball of soap there by the rock," she pointed.

"That would be fine," he answered. "How is your hand?"

"The cold water helped it some. Mayhap it is just badly bruised or sprained," said she as she entered the wooded wild berry patch.

Several minutes later she called softly, "Will! Shall I come back now?"

"Yes," he answered dejectedly.

"See the lovely berries. Wasn't the water refreshing?" she chattered. "Will, what is wrong? Why are you so glum?"

"When I went back up to the top, I found exactly what I feared I would. The horses who passed us last night left very clear prints in the sandy soil. There were little "S" prints from their shoes. They were definitely from the castle. Father is the only one for miles who has special shoes made for his horses. They search for me yet." He shook his head.

Now it was Hannah's turn to be the encourager. She placed her good hand on his arm. "Do not fear, my husband-to-be. The Lord is with us, and we need not be afraid. Here, turn your back and eat these berries. I will dress myself and we will be off on our journey."

Before she walked away from him, Will hugged her to himself fiercely. He had to struggle against the urges within him, so soft and sweet-smelling was she. He ran his hands through the long damp brown curls and choked out, "Do not braid it again, Hannah. You look so lovely with it down."

"As you wish," she agreed as she walked toward the bushes. "I could not braid it with one hand anyway. Hide your eyes."

He turned to douse the fire and brush away the remains of their lunch site.

Refreshed, they headed toward the afternoon sun.

Chapter 6

s the ox cart jostled along, Will could not resist taking the hand of his beloved when he spoke. "Can you believe how good our fortune has been since that awful day of your fall? Can it be only three weeks ago?"

Hannah delighted in his touch but only let herself relax when she had stolen a glance over her shoulder. Though it seemed to her that all the world must be staring at their entwined fingers, she could see that the servant boy who drove the cart was so lost in thought he would not look back.

Hannah and Will sat on the back of the cart with their legs dangling like school children. Between them and the driver were several urns of various sizes, full of goats' milk. In between and around all the urns was as much ice as could be spared from Frau Hohenburger's ice house. The servant boy constantly urged the team of oxen forward, lest all the ice melt in the unseasonably warm temperature.

"Ah, Will," the girl responded. "'Twas more than luck or good fortune that led us to Frau Hohenburger. 'Twas the very providence of God himself."

Together they reminisced over how they had literally stumbled into Frau's yard, so bone weary that they had not even noticed that a farm was nigh. It was three days after Hannah's fall and her hand had been painfully swollen. The day had been a rainy, dreary one, making it hard for Will to chart their course, for they followed the sun westward.

Now, Hannah laughed. "Remember how we practically ran right into her before we saw her that day? In all my born days, I've never seen such a wee bit of a woman."

"Nor a kinder, more wonderful example of Christian charity in action," Will responded.

In truth, Hannah and Will knew not what a pathetic sight they had made as they stumbled along in the rain that day. Their clothing was torn and tattered and soaked through. Their faces were gaunt and their eyes listless. Frau Hohenburger believed she had only done what any God-fearing person would do, but of course, she had done much more.

She had been making her way to the barn to do the afternoon milking of her 23 goats when she saw the forlorn pair stumbling across her barnyard.

"You there," she had called. The startled couple nearly jumped into the air. "Aach! 'Tis an awful rain to be traveling in. Whyn't you come inside to warm yourselves, children?" She bustled towards them, her goats forgotten for the time being.

Inside, Hannah thought she had never seen a cozier kitchen. There were cupboards all along the wall opposite the huge field stone fireplace. They had been built from planks of pine, and the knots in the wood had not been removed or worked around as was the usual practice with pine. Instead, the planks—knots and all—had been rubbed and oiled so many times that one could almost see one's own reflection in them. In the middle of the wall of cupboards was a window covered by yellow gingham curtains. The whole room radiated light in spite of the stormy weather, the effect being enhanced by several lighted tapers in wall sconces as well as oil lamps and the lighted fireplace. Hannah's heart so craved beauty that she noticed all this at a glance.

As she and Will sank into the chairs at the table, the Frau bustled about placing hot bowls of stew before them along with warm slabs of bread and a crock of butter. The aroma of the stew was permeating the kitchen so completely that immediately the young pair's mouths began to water and their stomachs growled within them. The butter had a different flavor than either of the travelers had ever tasted. It was so rich as it melted down through the delicious wheat bread. Will had buttered six slices for himself before pronouncing that he was "completely full and deeply grateful." Later they would learn that this meal had been their first introduction to the wonderful flavor of goat's milk and products made from it. 'Twas a flavor they would cherish in their future lives, and one that would ever bring to mind this haven from the storms of life.

Looking back, Hannah blushed at how she and Will had behaved that day. For they both devoured every morsel in sight with hardly a word passing between their lovely little gray-haired hostess and themselves.

When their immediate need for food had been met, Will began to speak. "Frau, let me express our thanks for a wondrous meal. I am Will Stevenson and this is my sister Harriet. We are traveling by foot to Amsterdam. Our parents recently died of the ague, and it was Mama's last wish that I take Harriet to her sister's home in Amsterdam till she comes of age."

Hannah stared at the floor during Will's gross deception.

Frau Hohenburger seemed hardly to hear him. "What happened to your hand, sweet?" she inquired, taking

Hannah's swollen hand into her own.

"I—I fell," Hannah mumbled.

"Let me make a plaster for it," their hostess said.

"I fear it is broken," Will interjected.

"Aach! No! See the fingers move freely. It is inflamed from all these cuts and snags. We may need to open it first."

Hannah shuddered involuntarily. Frau Hohenburger placed a hand on Hannah's forehead.

"Aach! The child is afire! We must get her into bed!"

The next three days were pretty much lost to Hannah. She vaguely remembered being bathed, bundled into a nightshirt and made to lie down amid the softest bed and the sweetest smelling sheets on earth. She now knew that sometime during those days Frau and Will had opened her hand to drain the poison. When she finally awoke, clear-headed, and free from pain, she bolted upright.

For a brief moment she wondered if she had died and entered heaven, for in the room where she found herself everything was white. The long window was surrounded by freshly starched and ironed white curtains edged in a lace pattern like one Hannah remembered watching her mother tat many years ago. The curtains were tied back at mid-length on the window with another strip of lace. Sunlight streamed through the window and fell on the white spread on top of the bed, as well as the walls in the room. Only the beautifully carved mahogany furniture offered contrast. The deep red-brown of the wood and all of the gleaming white could have been her introduction to her eternal home and Hannah would not have been disappointed. But . . . she was confused.

"Where am I? Will?" she shouted.

"Ah—finally!" The Frau had bustled into the room carrying a big glass of goat's milk. "It is mighty sick you have been. Drink this," she ordered.

Hannah obeyed. "Uh—my brother, Will—where is he?" she mumbled with downcast eyes.

"Miss Hannah, Sir William is in the barn helping me with my goats. You needn't keep up the pretense any longer. Your young man told me the whole truth the first night you were here. And a good thing he did. The very next morning two riders from the castle came here asking of him. Will hid in the hay and I told them you were my sick daughter. You needn't fear any more, for the older rider—whom Will said was his brother—said they may as well head back to the castle and proclaim Sir William dead!"

All the while she spoke, Frau had been ministering to Hannah's needs, changing her gown, brushing her tangled hair, bathing her face.

"But what of your family, sweet? Shouldn't we notify them that you are safe?" the old lady asked.

When Hannah explained what her home life had been like, the subject was dropped and never touched upon again.

Frau insisted they stay with her until Hannah regained her strength. The many plasters did their work of healing and soon Hannah's hand was almost as good as new. Only the cut and the stitches remained sore.

Will had been delighted with his work these past weeks for he had helped Frau's servants get a crop of winter wheat planted. Hannah had helped Frau with the goats and household chores. Frau had no money to pay them for their labor but she insisted on paying.

As it turned out, she paid them in things far more valuable to the travelers than money would have been.

On the other side of Will, as the wagon jostled along, sat a valise filled with some of their pay. The rest was in a box next to Hannah. It seemed Frau Hohenburger's sister had recently passed away. Unlike the Frau, the sister must have been nearly identical to Hannah in size. So Frau had given Hannah all of her dead sister's clothing. Never before had Hannah felt so rich. She remembered how she had cried tears of gratitude at the abundance. Five dresses, a shawl, a strong pair of shoes, and lots of underthings! And nothing was tight across her chest. What freedom of movement she had! This was surely heaven.

Will likewise had been outfitted with some fresh clothing—hand-me-downs from the servant boy's father, mostly. Not as wonderful as Hannah's new treasures—but serviceable.

Next to Hannah sat their other payment for the little work they had done for Frau Hohenburger. It was a box with foodstuff—enough to last them to Amsterdam if they were careful. Of course, it all had to be of the type which would keep—lots of garden truck, some goats' milk cheese, fudge made of the same substance, and some chicken and squirrel which had been fried. After all the rabbits and fish, these would be real treats.

Perhaps their best payment for their stay with the Frau had been in memories. Their lives had fit together in beautiful harmony. They had shared their hopes and fears. They had sung and laughed together. Each evening they read the Bible and had evening prayers together. Their time in Frau's house had given Hannah a beautiful glimpse of her future life with Will, one she would cherish often during the long hard months to come.

Hannah would have liked to stay on longer with the Frau—perhaps even forever as Frau had suggested. But grateful though Will was, he seemed driven to his dream of America. And so, early this morning, they had said their farewells.

Frau sent the cart each Friday to a distant farm where a young boy lived who could not seem to digest any milk but that from goats. The boy's farm was just across the border in Holland.

A tear slid down Hannah's cheek as she picked up some knitting needles. Frau Hohenburger had warned Hannah often that she'd best keep that sore hand busy, else it would stiffen on her. This morning as they climbed aboard the back of the ox cart, she had thrust the needles and a ball of beautiful soft white yarn into her hands. "Knit as ye go. Make ye something to remember Frau Hohenburger by when ye come into the fair land of America. May God go with ye always, as doth my love."

"I wonder if we shall ever see her again, Will," Hannah choked as the tears fell unashamedly now.

"I know not about on this earth," he replied. "But, thanks be to Jesus, we certainly will see her again in glory."

"Hey, Mister," the servant boy shouted. "See them 'ere hills back by them trees? Ye be a-lookin' at the hills of Holland now. Ye've left Germany."

Will pulled his legs up in the wagon and leaned against the low side. He turned his face forward.

"I don't want to be seeing the past. Somewhere out there lies a big ocean. Across it is our home. Our future lies in America."

Chapter 7

s it? Can it possibly be? Whispered Hannah as she stared off at the horizon. "Are we finally finished walking, Will? she sighed.

"Aach! My lady, me thinks you will live to regret those words. The day may come, and not too far in the future, when we are on a boat out on that water when you will wish you could walk about more. My Uncle Henry oft used to talk of the cramped quarters on a ship, and how he enjoyed the freedom of movement on land."

"Mayhap you are right, my dear," she answered. "But just now it feels so wonderful to just sit. It seems forever to me since we started our journey. How long has it been?"

"We left home five weeks and three days ago. Considering the three weeks spent with dear Frau Hohenburger, our travel time is nothing short of miraculous. I never hoped to make it this quickly. Hannah, you have been such a good soldier. I pray I have not pushed you too hard."

"Oh Will, don't be such a worrier. I am bone-tired, 'tis true. But it is a good kind of tired, for we are in Amsterdam, and we have completed the first leg of our journey to freedom."

She sighed as she breathed deeply of the salt air. "'Tis a lovely quiet sea, isn't it?" They both leaned against the trunk of a huge tree and stared at the evening beauty as the orange ball of fire slid into the water. Hannah closed her eyes and Will hummed a lovely hymn.

"God has been so good to us," he began. "It seems He has led us to just the right people all along—ever since the Frau, hasn't He?"

They sat thus and reminisced over their trip for a long time. Hannah's lovely laughter rang out over the water as they spoke of the tall thin man who gave them a ride all day in his buggy.

"I wonder if he ever ate a square meal. He was so thin even his pince-nez could not stay atop his nose. Remember how he chided us to be wary of the poisonous snakes and heavy branches that might fall on us out of the trees as we stepped out of the buggy that day?"

Will chuckled. "Yes, I'm sure 'twas worry that kept him so thin. But even that worrisome attitude of his worked in our favor. For remember he said he would have worried the rest of his life had he let a pretty young lassie like you continue to walk in his presence."

"Well, I am not the only one who found a champion for my cause," she retorted with a giggle. "What about Fraulein Heldegarde?"

Will grimaced. "You lied to her so beautifully about me being your uncle whose wife had died last year. I'm sure the only reason her mother let us sleep in their barn that night is because she hoped she had at long last found a person of the male species who she could hook up with her darling Heldy. Ugh!"

"At least it got us a wonderful big breakfast that next morning. I wonder if she would have fed us so well had she known that you are not really available for dear *big* Heldegarde!"

Their laughter echoed back to them from the ocean. Heldegarde had been exactly equal in height and width. Her weight must have equaled that of two men. Will's eyes stole a glance at Hannah's lovely figure.

Suddenly she sat up straight. "Remember Brother Benjamin? Of all my memories of this journey I hope the Lord shall always help me to maintain a clear remembrance of Brother Ben."

Together they smiled as they thought of the lovely old Jewish man who had shared his meager meal with them night before last. He still kept every law and ordinance as ordained by Moses all those thousands of years before. He was eagerly awaiting the birth of his Messiah. How their hearts ached for him to know that Messiah had already come. But in spite of their disagreement over Jesus, Brother Ben had been so kind to them. He had encouraged Hannah to do their necessary washing in the stream behind his house. And he'd insisted on her sleeping on his cot while he joined Will on the floor.

"We must always remember to pray for Benjamin. And for all the others who helped us on our way. But, Hannah, we have forgotten the time. We should eat ere night completely falls."

They roasted the big fish Will had purchased in the Amsterdam market on a crude spit over their fire.

Both felt a bit nostalgic as they realized this could be their last night together alone on this trip. Tomorrow, Will would try to book their passage on a boat to America.

After they'd eaten their fill and Will had banked the fire, they walked along the shore a ways, sharing their hopes and dreams. Hannah was glad they had chosen to walk outside the city. On other nights she had shunned, indeed feared, privacy—tonight she craved it.

At length their legs gave out and they returned to their fire.

"Will, darling, I have something for you," she said.

"What is it? How can you possibly . . .?"

But before he could protest any further, she had reached into her valise and brought out the gift. She laid it in his hand.

Will was spellbound as he stared at the most beautiful white mittens he'd ever beheld. The finest silk at Stivers' Castle could not compare with what Hannah's own two hands had wrought.

"My Lady, I am undone. The Frau meant for you to make yourself something with that wool, I am certain!"

"She never specified. She just said to busy my hands with the knitting. I wanted to make them for you, and I know she would be pleased," Hannah argued. "But, do they fit? I tried to judge by how much bigger your hand was than mine, from the times when you've held it," she smiled.

He put them on. "Perfect!" he exclaimed. "Oh Hannah, I know hours of work have gone into these. Hours when mayhap I thought you slept as I did." She nodded sheepishly. "How can I ever thank you, My Lady?" He choked with emotion.

"Will," she began quietly, "I know we agreed not to worry o'er the future. And we promised not to speak of the days ahead when we will almost certainly be apart from each other. But I just wanted you to have these mits to remember me by during these uncertain days ahead of us."

Now there were tears on her cheeks, but she went on unashamedly. "I have learned to love you and depend on you so much, my darling, in these weeks and I must admit I greatly fear the future. But whatever happens, Will, you keep the mits near you and remember they were knitted by the girl who loves you with all her heart and waits to become your wife."

"Oh Hannah!" was all Will could manage to say. But his passionate embrace and kisses in the firelight told her all she longed to know. It was the one and only time since their departure on the journey that their longing for each other almost overtook their principles. But though they loved deeply, they loved God deeper still.

So, after a time of recommitment to each other and to their future dreams, Hannah and Will fell asleep as always, holding hands.

When she awoke, Hannah was chilled and sore from the cold hard ground. Will was nowhere to be seen, but she had just changed into the brown dress from the Frau and rebraided her hair when she heard him calling her name excitedly.

"Hannah! Hannah! Get up! Where are you? I've done it! We can go! Hannah?"

When she emerged from the group of fir trees that served as her boudoir, he grabbed her and swung her in a circle till she grew dizzy.

"Will, darling! Put me down!" she giggled. "What have you done?"

"We must hurry!" he exclaimed as he picked up their valises. "We are to leave for America this very day—in fact, this very hour! The ship is called the *Wedgewood*. She is an English vessel. The captain seems a good man, though the sailors are a rowdy lot. I have here the contract of our indentured servitude. As we are both young and strong, we will only have to work four years for our freedom. Hurry up, dear!"

How Hannah wished she could share Will's excitement as they entered the city. But it seemed every ounce of her being recoiled from what lay ahead of them. All Will could see was their freedom four long years in the future, and all she could see was the wonderful five weeks they'd had together.

Will pulled her up the precarious-looking plank to the deck of the ship. Reluctantly, Hannah held back, so that Will turned around and urged, "Hurry, Hannah! They are ready to sail."

"It smells," Hannah whimpered, holding a hankie to her nose.

"Aye. She stinks for certain," a brawny sailor laughed. "To landlubbers, 'tis a horrid stench, but to me, 'tis the air of heaven."

"It's the fish being hauled over there," Will pointed to a neighboring vessel. Hannah wondered where the other passengers were. Everyone she could see was working with ropes and sails and rigging. Almost as soon as they were aboard, the ship began to move. The captain was busy shouting orders to the muscular sailors and she felt very much in the way standing on the deck next to Will. The captain expertly maneuvered the ship between others held at anchor in the bay. When finally they were on the open sea, with the shore ever diminishing behind them, he approached them.

"Well, Stivers, I thought you weren't going to make it back aboard afore we sailed. So, this is your sister, eh? Well, we will get her settled with the other girl servants. Yer lucky, lassie. There be eight of ye this time. Last trip there was only one woman aboard. 'Twas a hard trip for her."

Hannah clung tightly to Will.

"Don't worry, lassie. Yer brother will be only a short distance from you in with the other men indentures. But ah, do ye want to say goodbye to the motherland?"

Hannah would have turned to gaze behind at Holland. But Will pulled her toward the front of the ship.

"Our home is out there, Hannah. No matter what happens, remember that I love you," he whispered in her ear.

Then the captain took them to their respective quarters.

Part 2

Voyage

Chapter 8

annah blinked repeatedly, trying to accustom herself to the dreary light of the cabin. Slowly, shadows seemed to emerge from the bunks lining the walls of the windowless room.

"This 'ere'll be your bunk, Missy Stivers." Hannah jumped as the captain came so close to calling her by the name she saved only for her dream life, but then she remembered. For the duration of the voyage she would be Will's sister!

The captain continued. "You can stow your gear in that 'ere box built into the wall. Your bunkie mate below you 'ere is Gretchen. The rest can introduce yourself. C'mon Will," he bellowed as he ducked back out through the door.

Hannah ran to the door to catch a last glimpse of Will but all she saw was his back as he entered another cabin doorway several yards away. As she slowly turned around, the girl named Gretchen spoke.

"Do you have a first name, Miss Stivers?"

Hannah suddenly grew shy. She dropped her head and mumbled, "Hannah."

"What? Speak up, lassie! You'll never get along being a servant in the new world if you can't make yourself heard! Now talk louder, or don't talk at all!" Shouted a gnarled old woman sitting on the only chair in the room. Hannah recoiled in fear. The speaker was the epitome of a witch out of fairy tales, right to the wart on the end of the nose.

"Oh, don't mind Grandmama. She's really not a bad old girl. She's just going deaf and it angers her so when she cannot hear," Gretchen reassured.

For some reason Hannah felt it was very important to win this old one's approval if the trip to America was to be even bearable. So she lifted her head and walked directly to the old lady's chair. She spoke slowly and much louder than normal.

"I said my name is Hannah, Ma'am. My brother and I will be indentured for four years in America. What is your name?"

The old lady cackled in delight. "See 'ere—the rest of ye—I'm not going deaf after all! I can hear this little thing perfectly. She speaks up clear-like. The rest of ye ought to take a lesson from 'er."

Now she addressed herself to Hannah. "The only name you need to know for me is Grandmama, understand? Me and my little Gretchen is leaving a very sad life behind us and we's leaving our names behind us, too. So, till we get to America and pick us out a new last name, we are just Grandmama and Gretchen. Got it?"

Hannah nodded as she began to put her belongings in the box on the wall. She wondered if every person on this boat was running away from something.

A gray-haired lady spoke from the bottom bunk just opposite Hannah's. "Pleased to meet you, Miss Hannah. I am Mistress Woodcutter, and these three are my daughters— Karla, Louisa and Marta. Say hello, girls."

The three little blondes dropped lovely curtsies at

Hannah's feet. But for the difference in their size they could have been triplets. Their lovely golden hair was in taut braids which fell past their waists. Their eyes were as blue as the morning sky in May and there was a smattering of golden freckles across their noses. They wore identical navy blue dotted swiss dresses covered by crisply starched aprons. They smiled shyly.

"Hello, little ladies. Aren't the three of you just about more beauty than your mother can handle? But, tell me, who is who? I don't know if I'll ever be able to tell you apart."

The tallest child spoke. "I'm Karla, and I am almost twelve years old. And the way to remember which of us is which is simple. We are alphabetical by age and height. Karla— 'K' is the eldest and tallest. 'L' for Louisa is next."

The second child interrupted with a shy grin. "I'm ten years old and I'm almost as tall as my sister." This last phrase was said on tiptoes as she craned her head as high as possible.

"And I'm Marta, and I'm only eight years old," spoke the third child dejectedly. She only came to Louisa's shoulder so there was no use trying to outdo her sisters.

Hannah sat down on the bunk below her own and pulled Marta to her. "And I think Marta is just about the prettiest name I've ever heard. To go with a very pretty little girl."

Marta hugged Hannah and said over her shoulder, "Oh Mama, I like this lady. She is already my friend."

Mistress Woodcutter told the girls to leave Hannah to her unpacking. Immediately they all three climbed onto the bunk above their mama's and began to play quietly with some dolls.

Hannah was surprised to see such lovely manners in servant children, and remarked the same to the mother.

"Oh Hannah, we are not servants."

Hannah flushed, "But, the captain said . . ."

"Oh, Captain Phillip again. He is such a teaser. You see, Hannah, he is my brother-in-law. My husband went to America nigh onto two years ago. He has built a large lumber business in the colony of Virginia. So, now that he is prospering, he sent word for us to come join him on the next trip the *Wedgewood* made. For some strange reason, Phillip has told everyone on ship that the girls and I are indentured servants like the rest of you when we really are his relation." Mistress Woodcutter tried to smile as she shook her head, but she did not succeed.

Hannah thought this was a strange thing for a man to tease about. Just as she had folded the last of her under-things and placed them in the box, the old lady bellowed.

"Gretchen, introduce her to Miz Planter. Time she quit her cry-babying anyway."

Hannah was surprised to see another occupant of the cabin, for she had supposed that last bunk to be empty. Now a tiny shadow half sat up and blew its nose.

Hannah walked over to the edge of the bed. A young woman stared at her through tear-filled eyes. "I'm Susan Planter," she choked. "My . . . my husband . . . he passed away last month . . . a hunting accident. I . . . I don't have no living relations 'cept an uncle and aunt in some town name of Boston in America. I don't have no money either so's all I knew to do to get to my uncle was to sell myself. Cap'n Woodcutter—he says I'll have to work six years to pay for this trip." Here she began to cry hard again. Hannah tried to comfort her when the sobbing turned to choking and wretching. She ran from the cabin.

The old lady shook her head. "Everyone knows women on ships is supposed to bring bad luck. But one who is about half way to term of delivering her first baby—that has got to be double bad luck!"

"Oh, Grandmama, don't!" Gretchen shouted. "I feel sorry for Miz Planter. I've never seen the equal of that woman's fear anywhere. She's more petrified of her future than I am of rats, and you know . . ." Her voice trailed off with an involuntary shudder.

Hannah thought she knew the feeling. The closeness of the cabin was beginning to bother her. She knew she would have to get used to it in the future, but just now she felt a desperate need for air.

"Are we allowed to walk about on the deck?" she asked.

"Why, of course, dear. You are a servant, not a slave!" Mistress Woodcutter responded. "If my head did not ache so, I would take the girls out for air myself."

"They may come with me," Hannah replied.

In a flash the four were all bundled in capes and fascinators and going out the door. "Only stay out of the sailors' way, pets," the mother warned.

Hannah scanned the deck hunting for Will. He was nowhere to be seen, but the mist had lifted, the ocean was smooth, the sky was bright, and it was a glorious day.

Karla, Louisa, and Marta kept a lively chatter going about all their Papa had written them from the new world. Hannah only half listened to them. She was entranced watching a sailor climb in the tall rigging when a familiar voice startled her.

"Are you all settled in, My Lady?"

Her heart skipped a beat. "Oh Will, I'm so glad to see you. Will we be able to meet and talk like this every day?"

"Well, I understand we are to be allowed a certain amount of freedom, as long as we stay out of the sailors' way. But who are these?"

Hannah blushed at her lack of manners. She introduced the girls, asked Karla to keep an eye on the others for a few minutes, and she and Will walked a few steps away.

"Is it going to be too horrible, my dear?" he asked, a deep concern gleaming in his eyes.

"Oh no," she responded. "It is not bad at all. I already

61

feel I know the other women. The old one called Grandmama will be trying, I fear. But these girls are sweet, and my bunk mate Gretchen seems amiable. Miz Planter is the one I fear for. She is pathetic. But what of your cabin? Is it crowded and dark?"

"Well, yes. But evidently only half as crowded as yours. There are two young boys. Were I a betting man I'd lay odds that they are running away from home. They wanted to hire on as sailors, but Cap'n didn't need them so they sold themselves as we did, for four years. The other man seems friendly, but he doesn't speak a word of German, and I no French, so we just smile and nod at each other."

She laughed, and he unthinkingly took her hand in his.

"Hello, Uncle Phillip," shouted Marta as she ran past Will and Hannah. Will immediately dropped her hand and turned to see the captain watching them intently.

The little girl clung to her uncle's leg. He brushed her aside gruffly. "Don't child. I only came out to ring the bell for the noonday meal." He spoke more to Will than to anyone else. "The first bell is for half the crew to eat. The second bell is the other half. And the third bell means you indentures can go to the galley and get whatever is left, take it to your cabins, and eat."

"Uncle Phillip, can we eat with you up here on deck?" Marta asked, as a steward brought the captain a tray.

"No," he replied. "You and your mother will eat with the other women below. And you best get out of the way now."

The three girls started for the cabin. "I'd better go with them," Hannah explained. "Will, I shall hope to see you at nooning—the third bell?" she smiled.

Will watched as she took Marta's hand and headed for the cabin. "Someday 'twill be our little one's hand she holds," he muttered.

Chapter 9

he next several days were very pleasant ones. While at times the size of the ship did seem to be a bit confining, all in all it was not too unpleasant. The height of Hannah's bunk had at first been a worry to her, but once she lay on the goose feather mattress, the height problem melted away.

Hannah seemed to flourish with the sea air and slept very well each night. During the daytime she explored the ship. The hold was full of all sorts and sizes of boxes. Some sailors told her they contained mostly farm implements to be sold in America. Hannah inspected the tiny galley, also down below, and found it spotlessly clean but inadequately stocked in her opinion. Up on deck again, one could walk all around the outside area of the ship; it was virtually empty. In the middle of the deck were all the masts and sail riggings. And of course, the "quarters." Toward the rear of the deck and up a flight of ten steps (which the sailors called a "ladder") was the wheelroom which led directly into the captain's quarters.

Hannah instinctively knew this area would be off limits, but through the tiny round windows she could see red

velvet draperies and she imagined Captain Phillip Woodcutter's abode to be very elegant. Here on the main deck
were the sleeping areas for the indentureds. Actually, the
ladies slept directly under the captain. Then there was a
narrow, dark hallway out of which opened the room
where Will slept. In the middle of the dark hallway were
the steps leading to the ship's hold, where Hannah presumed
the crew slept among the boxes of cargo. It didn't take
long for Hannah to learn all about the ship's routine, when
and where she was welcome, and what she was expected
to do.

There was just enough wind to keep the ship moving
along at a nice pace, but not enough to make the crossing
too rough. All the ladies worked together to try to improve
Miz Planter's spirits, and Hannah truthfully told Will, "I
think she is finally coming out of the depths of despair.
It is so wonderful to see her begin to take an interest in
life again. We even talked her into eating last evening, for
the baby's sake. The Lord is truly answering our prayers
on her behalf."

Will chuckled. "I don't know if it is an improvement
for one to begin eating this food or not."

Mealtimes were a constant source of irritation to all the
passengers. They could understand the need for the crew
to eat first. But twice in this first week at sea, the third
bell had never been rung because there was no food left.
Will said the food was so horrid he did not miss it. Truly,
it left a lot to be desired, but Hannah knew that they must
eat to keep their strength up. So daily she prayed that
the crew would not be quite so hungry.

It had been Grandmama's idea to get Miz Planter's mind
off herself and onto the new baby. Thus each of the women
had donated one of their softest nicest undergarments for
baby clothing. The old lady supervised as they cut out
baby shirts and gowns. Even the three little girls had joined

64

in the proceedings. They each tore lace and bows from a few of their many clothes to donate to "the baby." Thus the tiny unborn child's wardrobe grew and with each stitch taken by lamplight in the dark cabin, friendships and understanding between the women strengthened.

They all joined together at the end of the second week in a colossal work day. The cook boiled water in the galley for them and they washed all their dirty garments. It seemed the entire hold of the ship was strung with clothesline as all day long the clothing dried.

Hannah had cared for Will's clothes also. It was as she was folding his shirts for him, that he entered the hold and found her all alone. "I give you my gratitude, my heart, and my life, dear Hannah," he mumbled in her ear as he hugged her from behind. For a moment she relaxed in his embrace. Then, sensing that she must help him restrain his longing, she whirled on him. Laughingly she said, "Why, brother dear, your washing is the least I can do for you." He took the shirts to his cabin, laughing all the way.

A few minutes later as Hannah was placing her clean clothing into the box, there was a knock on the cabin door. All the ladies were startled to see the red-faced captain's steward when Gretchen opened the door.

"Cap'n Phillip—uh, he wants to see Miss Stivers in his cabin up topside quick!"

An unknown fear clutched at Hannah's heart as she followed the steward. What could this mean? As she entered the captain's quarters, which were indeed nicely furnished, but nothing nearly so grand as Hannah had imagined, she saw Will facing the awesome man.

The captain's face was so red and contorted with obvious rage that Hannah dropped her eyes to the floor, staring at the red carpeting with gold eagles on it.

"Why weren't the two of you truthful with me?" he bellowed.

"What do you mean, sir?" responded Will.

"Aw Stivers, do ye think I am a blind man? This lassie is not your sister and we both know it!"

"But, Captain, I . . ." Will hesitated. Hannah trembled beside him. What would be the outcome of their sin? Vaguely, she remembered the story of Jonah and a whale. Would this man throw them overboard?

"Mr. Stivers, there is no law against a man and his wife traveling together. If I'd known the two of you were wed, I would've granted ye a common cabin. Why on earth didn't ye want me to know?"

"But sir, we are not man and wife," Hannah answered.

"Do not lie to me again," he barked. "I've suspicioned from the first day aboard that ye were no siblings. I've never seen a brother and sister yet look at each other with the moon all over their faces as ye two do. And just now one of the sailors saw ye hugging in the hold. I'm askin' ye again, man—why are ye keeping yer marriage a secret?"

Will's head dropped. "Cap'n Woodcutter, there has been no marriage. Hannah is my betrothed, but we are not yet wed."

Now the captain's face grew florid. "I'll not have adultery aboard my ship, man!" he screamed.

At the word "adultery," Hannah snapped to attention. Her face was purple with shame but in a very controlled voice she said, "Captain Woodcutter, that is not true. I shall accept your apology before 'tis even given.

"'Tis true, William and I committed a sin to lie to you. But we have never, nor ever shall, commit the sin you just named. We love each other, and yes—we've been traveling together these seven weeks now but we've not done anything I'd be ashamed to tell my mother, God rest her soul. William is a gentleman and I a lady—and we've not known each other!" Having spoken, Hannah heaved a hugh sigh of relief.

Will was watching her, and his eyes glowed with pride. Now he turned back to the captain. "What she says is true."

Captain Phillip Woodcutter was embarrassed. "Well, on my word, Stivers—why don't ye marry this pretty little thing? I'm a ship's captain on the high seas. Don't you know I can make your union legal? I—uh, . . . I'll even let you use my cabin here for your honeymoon. Just let me clean up a bit and we'll marry up the two of ye, post haste."

Hannah thought her heart had stopped beating. *Oh— please, God*, she pleaded silently, *let Will agree with the captain.*

The room was silent for a long time. Hannah hoped; Will wrestled within himself. Finally he spoke, so quietly that Hannah had to strain to hear every word.

"Sir, can you guarantee me that when we get to America, Hannah and I would be sold together for the four years?"

"Well, no. But there's always a chance," the captain replied.

"I cannot take that chance, sir. It will be terrible to be separated for that long anyway. But, if we were wed, I know I could not bear it." As he spoke his eyes lifted to hers. Her heart wrenched to see that they were wet with tears.

The captain sat at his big desk shaking his head. "Stivers, I admire your principles. But I think ye are a fool. I'll try to keep your secret. But the two of ye had better be more careful." He smiled, and Hannah realized it was the first she'd ever seen a smile light his face. He was really quite handsome. "'Tis a mighty strange brother and sister who hug and hold hands and even try to steal a kiss. Be more careful. Dismissed!" he said gruffly.

Hannah motioned for Will to leave. When the captain supposed they both had fled, he was surprised to look up and see Hannah still there.

"Sir, I feel compelled to ask you. Why are you so stern and horrid to your brother's wife and children? Little Marta loves you so much and Mistress Woodcutter . . ."

He slammed his fist on the desk. "Miss Stivers—or who- ever ye really are—ye are dismissed! My relationship with my sister-in-law is none of your concern. I've agreed to keep your secret. Now don't push me, young lady!"

Hannah ran all the way back to the cabin.

That very night the storm hit. Marta's screams woke Hannah, but as she opened her eyes she had to grab the frame of the bed to keep from falling out. Their cabin seemed to be pitching to nearly forty-five degree angles. It was so dark, and they dare not light a candle for fear of fire, but Hannah soon determined that all eight of them were awake and petrified. Karla was trying to calm Louisa. Gretchen was sitting on Grandmama's bunk trying to keep her from being slammed around too much. And poor Miz Planter was being sick—violently so. Their door was slamming open when they tipped one way and shut when the ship rolled back. On the "open" rolls, they could see lightning and hear the crewmen yelling about securing ropes and bailing. On the "shut" rolls, all they could hear was terrible thunder, a horribly violent wind, Marta's cries, and poor Miz Planter.

Hannah tried to minister to her needs, but soon it was not just Miz Planter who needed help. The violent tossing combined with the horrible stench in the room. It seemed Hannah and Gretchen were the only seaworthy sailor women aboard the *Wedgewood*. The ladies and girls groaned and moaned between sieges of violent illness. Hannah and Gretchen spent what seemed like hours sliding and stumbling from one bunk to the next holding weary heads and trying to clean soiled clothing and bedding.

When Hannah could sense that daylight was approach- ing, she pulled on a dress overhead. She knew that she had reached her limit both emotionally and physically. Leaving Gretchen in charge of the sick ones, she ran out on the deck to seek help. She had to hold with all her might to the rigging, masts, anything she came across to keep from being thrown overboard. She shouted her need of help, but the wind carried her words away. Just as she was about to despair, she plunged headlong into a man.

"Oh, Captain sir, they are so sick! Is there a doctor? What can I do?"

"You little fool! Get back to your cabin and stay there, that's what! Over half my crew is just as sick as you women! I cannot help!"

"But, Captain, the smell! Is there nothing—?"

Now he forcefully took her arm and pulled her into the narrow hallway, out of the main force of the wind. "Can't you understand, Miss Hannah? The only help I can offer you is water. There's plenty of that, everywhere! And if you don't get back to your cabin so I can get back to the wheel, the *Wedgewood* may flip in these seas and then a little smell would be the least of your worries. For the second time in one day I tell you—dismissed!"

Hannah ran for the cabin, going past the men's cabin on the way. She hesitated, and as the ship tossed, their door flew open also.

"Will, are you alright?" she screamed.

She heard his feeble moans in reply, and knew that her darling had also succumbed to seasickness.

Not too far from the door to the women's cabin stood a huge water barrel. When she found she couldn't budge the barrel—*So this is why everything is fastened down on the ship*, she thought—she and Gretchen took turns struggling to the barrel and back with pitchers of water. Most of it spilled en route, 'tis true, but it still helped to be able to rinse off soiled faces and hands with a cool splash.

The tossing continued all day and into the next. No

bells were sounded, for no one dared think of food. When at last there was no one still wretching, Hannah and Gretchen stripped all the sheets off the bunks and stuffed them into the nearly empty water barrel outside. The six ladies lay whimpering into the night. Hannah fell, exhausted, onto a bunk that still rolled. Soon she was asleep, in spite of herself.

She never knew for sure how long she slept. She only knew that when she awoke, the door to the cabin was being held ajar. Grandmama was on her knees scrubbing the floor with a strong lye soap. "You stay put and rest ye, Missy. You've surely earned a sleep. If 'tweren't for you, I think as that we'd all of died in that storm."

Hannah sat up and rubbed her eyes. Marta was the only other still in bed, and Mistress Woodcutter sat at her side placing cool cloths on her head. But for them, the room was empty. Hannah's confusion showed on her face.

"Captain's orders," said the mother. "Everyone is topside breathing fresh air and eating crackers. But Marta is still too sick."

After Hannah had freshened herself a bit, she too went above. It was a glorious day—bright sunshine and just a few white clouds. Some sailors were mending a torn sail. Others were swabbing the deck. She blinked in the bright sunlight.

There was Will, with a blonde healthy looking child on each hand.

"We've been telling your brother here how wonderful you were, taking care of all of the rest of us!" Louisa exclaimed.

"Are you alright?" she asked. He was white as a ghost, except around his mouth, and that area looked green.

"I think I'll live—now that the boat no longer tosses. I believe you are the better sailor in our family, right, sis?" He winked. "Here, have a cracker!"

Chapter 10

he days grew monotonous.

As Will had predicted six weeks earlier, the day did come when Hannah longed for more room to move about than the boat afforded. She remembered the long days walking through the hills of Germany and would have given anything to plant her feet on solid soil again. But at least there had been no more storms. For that she was thankful.

"But why doesn't Marta get well?" Mistress Woodcutter asked that evening. "The rest of us all got over our bout with seasickness long ago. But poor dear Marta still can't keep anything down. What is wrong with her?"

Though spoken in the crowded cabin, the question went unanswered, for there just did not seem to be any answers.

In the two weeks prior to the storm, Marta had made friends of everyone on board ship. During that fair weather period she had spent countless hours on deck with her sisters. They had played hopscotch or jack stones or frolicked in a land of make-believe with their dolls. Karla and Louisa were often heard arguing. They were so near of a size to one another that there had grown a strong competition between the two. But Marta was ever the peacemaker. The youngest of the three, she often seemed to possess the most common sense. When an argument arose, she often had changed the subject. Thus, while all three girls were petted and spoiled by the crew, Marta had quickly become everyone's sweetheart. So her illness seemed to affect the entire ship.

"How's the lassie today?" asked one big burly Irishman, as he pushed the mop of unruly red hair out of his eyes. Hannah shook her head sadly and the man blew his nose. "Such a sweet one she is. I've got me a daughter just about her age at home. It lessened me longin' for m' little Katie the other week when I played a game of checkers with little Marta. I'm a prayin' to the Holy Mother and blessed Saint Christopher for her all the time. Let me know, Miss Hannah, if there's a thing Big Mac can do to help the lassie!"

He was no more than gone when another of the crew members came to the door. Hannah had never spoken to this young fellow before. He seemed well educated, though he stuttered quite severely.

"Is th-there an-an-any impr-improvem-ment in the t-t-tiny ch-child y-yet?" he asked.

Hannah saw such longing in the youth's pimply face that she could not bear to dash his hopes as she had Big Mac's. "Well, she is no worse today. No better," she added, "but no worse."

The gangly boy's eyes were wet. "Sh-she re-re-reminds me of m-my lit-little sister."

Hannah tried to draw him out of his shell. "How old is your sister?"

He shook his head sadly. "She w-would have b-b-been s-s-six, b-but she died in the s-same f-fire that k-killed my m-mother and f-father. W-well, I have to go b-back up in the s-sails, but I h-hope sh-she gets w-well."

As he began to leave Hannah called, "Please pray for her."

He turned to face Hannah again, unashamed of the tears now. 'W-we have been, l-lady. A b-bunch of the b-boys and m-me're all pr-praying."

A steady stream of the crew members came and went silently. On and on it went. One brought a little string toy he had fashioned for Marta. Each sailor expressed his love and concern in his own way. These big gruff men were reduced to putty in the hands of the little blonde girl. The cook even improved his fare, bringing special broths and puddings to try to tempt her to eat.

A day finally came when Hannah was able to tell Will in one of her brief visits to the deck that it looked as if prayer was being answered, for Marta was rallying a bit. The news spread like wildfire on the ship and everyone seemed in a jubilant mood.

But the next day Marta was sick again, now worse than before. Eventually everyone had to admit that this was more than mere motion sickness. About a week after the storm Marta began to run a fever. It was slight at first, just enough to cause her head to ache. But as day stretched after day, the fever began to visibly increase and take its toll. She was often out of her head, screaming for Papa to run from the bears. When she was lucid, she lay limp and whimpered, "Mama, what is wrong with me?" The ladies took turns sitting at her side replacing the cold cloths as they grew steamy from the hot little brow. Karla and Louisa spent most of their time on deck, as everyone wondered if Marta's illness were contagious. Sometimes Hannah didn't know who she pitied the most, the sick child or the two healthy ones. For it was obvious that when they accidentally began to enjoy themselves, they immediately felt guilty and stopped.

It was Hannah's turn to stay with Marta one afternoon. She pulled a stool close to Marta's bedside and sat down upon it, pulling a tiny book from her apron pocket. She had

73

begun to spend her watching time in reading her little New Testament, a precious gift from Frau Hohenburger.

"What are you reading?" asked Karla, startling Hannah.

"I'm reading from the Gospel of John in the Bible."

"Papa reads the Bible to us. Will you read it to me?" came the answer.

The girl sat cross-legged on the floor at Hannah's feet, leaning back against her sister's bunk. So Hannah began to read the beloved story. When she came to that most loved verse of all in chapter three she hesitated. Smiling, she read, "For God so loved Karla Woodcutter that he gave his only Son."

"It doesn't say that!" interrupted the girl.

"But it means that. God loves you so much that if you'd been the only person on earth He still would have sent Jesus to die for you."

"Does He love Marta, too?" asked the girl.

"Oh yes," Hannah responded. "In fact, He loves her so much that I wouldn't be surprised if He might take her to live with Him soon."

Karla's eyes stood full of tears. "I don't want her to die," she choked. "But I don't want her to have to hurt so much either."

"We can pray for her," Hannah replied. Together they asked God to take care of Marta and do whatever was best for her.

Even Hannah was surprised when Karla added to her prayer, "And Jesus, make Uncle Phillip love us again." Hannah's heart broke at the innocent request. No one had guessed how hard the captain's treatment had hurt the little girls.

Later that day the ship seemed to enter a giant calm. The wind slackened and finally died completely. The sails dropped and the ship did not move at all.

The sunset was lovely. It began with vivid orange in

74

the middle and went through nearly every color of the rainbow before becoming deep purple on the outer edges.

Just as the huge orange ball was sinking into the westernmost edge of the sea, there was a timid knock at the cabin door. An audible gasp escaped Mistress Woodcutter's lips when Hannah opened the door.

"May—uh, may I see my niece?" said the captain as he stared at the floor with his hat in his hands.

Everyone moved aside, but no one spoke. Perhaps it was the sudden quiet that awakened the child. Sweat stood out on her little brow as she tried to sit up, but fell back in utter exhaustion.

"Uncle! Uncle Phillip—you came!" she squeaked.

In a flash he was on his knees at her bedside. With arms around her, he faced her mother. "I've been a fool—a crazy old fool," he confessed. Holding the child at arm's length he said, "Your mother and I argued over whether she should pay for your trip on my ship. I was so proud, I didn't want to accept the money from her, even though I need it. But I was wrong. And I shouldn't have held it against you children. Forgive me, please all of you."

As he spoke Marta began to cough violently. There was blood in the mucus that came up.

Mistress Woodcutter took her in her arms. She placed her hand on the captain's. "It's alright, Phil. I know all about the Woodcutter men and their pride. I was wrong, too." Together they embraced Marta, who had fallen asleep again.

"She's just got to get well!" he mumbled as he left the cabin.

Late that evening as the huge yellow moon shown down on the glassy mirror of the sea, little Marta's tired heart stopped beating. By the time Karla and Louisa awoke, some of the sailors had already built a strong little coffin for her to be placed in.

Captain Phillip Woodcutter was so overcome with grief and remorse that it fell to his sister-in-law to comfort him. "If only I had come to her earlier—before she had grown so weak—maybe . . ." he sobbed.

But the tired mother corrected him. "No, Phil, don't do this to yourself. Her illness had nothing to do with you. Mayhap . . . she might have even grown ill and passed on had we been on land. At least . . . at least she died knowing that all was forgiven 'twixt us. And we will see her again in heaven someday." At this, Mistress Woodcutter broke into sobs. They clung to each other in grief.

The sea was still perfectly quiet. The captain, the mother, and two sisters stood hand in hand as four of the biggest sailors carried the pine box to the bow of the ship. The entire crew and all the passengers stood with heads bowed as Will Stivers read from the same Gospel Hannah had read to Karla.

"In my Father's house are many mansions: if it were not so, I would have told you. I go to prepare a place for you. And if I go and prepare a place for you, I will come again, and receive you unto myself; that where I am, there ye may be also."

Even Will's strong voice broke several times as he prayed that God would comfort this grieving family with the thought that little Marta was now running through the streets of heaven.

Hannah thought she had never heard a more final sound than the splash as the little box containing the earthly body of Marta was dropped into the sea.

Almost within the hour, from out of nowhere, a breeze began to blow. The sailors immediately jumped to their respective tasks. But as the *Wedgewood* finally began to move again, two little girls with braids to their hips stood at the stern of the ship and stared into the depths where their sister had been buried. If they were in the way, no one told them so.

Everyone feared for Karla and Louisa's health. The captain ordered all of the bed things used by the sick child to be burned. Day followed anxious day, but no one else became ill and the whole ship's company relaxed.

With the passing of time passengers and crew members adjusted to the loss of Marta in their own way. One day as Hannah was watching the girls play on deck, Big Mac stopped in front of her. He carried a huge coil of rope over one of his big arms, and pushed the red hair out of his eyes with the other hand.

"Miss Hannah, will you give the girls' mother a message for me?" he asked.

"Surely," Hannah replied. "What is it?"

"Doubt it will help her much," he mumbled. "But I want her to know that her wee one did not die in vain. Me wife has been a beggin' me to give up the life of the sea 'ere since m' Katie was a tiny baby. Says she needs me to home. Now—seing how quick-like a child can be taken—well, I've made m' decision. This'll be m' last voyage. When I get me home to Ireland, I'll be home for good."

"That's wonderful," Hannah nodded. "I shall tell the mistress." But Hannah knew Mistress Woodcutter was not yet ready to accept that any good thing could have come from losing Marta, so she decided to keep the confidence buried in her heart and bring it out at the appropriate time.

Late that afternoon two teary-eyed girls sought the comfort of Hannah who was reclining against a barrel on the foreward deck. "What is it? Are you feeling sick?" Hannah asked fearfully.

"No, Miss Hannah. We were just talking," Louisa began but broke off as Karla interrupted.

"I was telling Louisa about that day before . . . before . . . you know . . . when you read to me out of the Bible. And we were talking about what your brother read at Marta's

". . . at Marta's . . ."

Now Louisa picked up the narrative. "And we were wondering . . . if we will really and truly ever . . . ever . . . see her again?" They both turned tear-filled, hopeless blue eyes on Hannah.

"Oh girls, sit down with me," Hannah choked as she pulled one down on each side of her. She fumbled in her pocket and found the little New Testament. "Let's see," she began in John 3 again. "Remember, Karla, I said God so loved the world—"

"No, you said He loved me and Marta!"

"What about me?" asked wide-eyed Louisa.

And so it was that Hannah was able to show two little girls how to ask Jesus into their lives and receive forgiveness of sins and the certainty of heaven. After each had prayed separately to receive Jesus, Hannah turned to the 14th chapter of John and they talked at length about heaven and how happy little Marta must be. Suddenly Karla's face clouded.

"Wait, Miss Hannah. I loved Marta—I still do—but she had done some bad things in her life, too. Mayhap she didn't get to go to heaven. Mayhap she's . . ."she shuddered.

"Oh no, Karla—that can't be. Now, listen very closely to me. Do you really think little Marta could have ever understood the verses we've read and the things we've talked about today?"

The girls were deep in thought for a few seconds. At almost precisely the same moment they shook their heads negatively. "Maybe she could have if we had been taught about this all the time. But since our daddy went to America we haven't read the Bible regularly or gone to church much. So—no," Karla said, "I think she was just too little to understand."

"That's right," Hannah replied. "And the Bible indicates in many places that children who die before they can understand God's plan of salvation and thus be held accountable for their sins go to heaven anyway. One place is in the Old Testament when King David's infant son died. David says, "I shall go to him." Another place is here in Matthew chapter 18 where Jesus said that in order to get to heaven we must become like little children."

Karla and Louisa both sighed contentedly. "So then we *will* see her again!"

"Yes!" Hannah assured them. After a few more minutes they ran off to play happily. Hannah bowed her head and silently thanked the Lord for the second good result she could attribute to Marta's passing in one day.

Grandmama soon began to worry and complain because Gretchen was often nowhere to be found. "Where does she spend all of her hours?" she bellowed.

No one had the courage to explain to the dear old lady what the entire ship, except she with her failing senses, had observed. Almost from the first day of their trip, Gretchen had been enamored by one of the "runaway" boys who shared the cabin with Will. In the early days, both boys had vied for her affection. But it soon became evident that Gretchen only had eyes for George, the older of the two. Proprieties were thrown to the wind and things that would have been called scandalous on land were actually encouraged by the people on the ship. Gretchen and George spent long hours talking to each other, learning all there was to know about the other. And if, as they strolled on the deck in the moonlight, they stole a little kiss, everyone chose to look the other way.

Finally, several weeks after Marta's passing, Gretchen fell on her knees in front of Grandmama. What should have been a private conversation was heard by everyone, due to the lady's deafness.

"I love him, Grandmama. We've gotten to know each other all these long weeks since we left home. He is to be indentured for four years, and then he wants to be a sailor."

The old lady shouted, "A sailor! He will leave you alone for years at a time. Ye'll be a widow before your time, girl. And anyway, we are under contract to work for six years!"

The youngster was patient. "I know, Grandmama. We've been through all that. George has even spoken to the captain about it. He says he cannot guarantee us we will be together, but he will try. But we don't care about that. We want to be married now. At least we can have all this next month or so before we get to America to be together. Please say you will give us your blessing."

Again the old lady remonstrated. "You are too young," she shouted with a violent wag of the head.

Gretchen had expected this argument and was evidently prepared for it. "How old were you when you married my grandfather?"

At this even Grandmama had to smile. "Well, I was a mite younger than you, but times were different back then. I . . . oh—what's the use? I can see you are determined. Well then, bring your young George in to meet his new grandmama. He'd better be good to you."

And so it was that all the ship was aflutter with the news of the approaching nuptials. The ladies had another colossal cleaning day, and once again the clotheslines crisscrossed the hold.

George and Will and two of the sailors set to work emptying a little storage room in the hold, cleaning it up, and preparing it as a honeymoon suite for the pair. While the captain and most of the crew griped about the bother caused by all these passengers—especially the women— Hannah knew that they too were glad for a break in their routine.

On the day of the wedding, Captain Woodcutter looked resplendent in his dress white uniform. Gretchen wore a lovely wool dress in a pale rose. Grandmama, who was sure she would catch pneumonia if she bathed, at least wore a clean apron to the ceremony. George looked spit-shined from the top of his orange hair to his tattered shoes. But Hannah couldn't keep her eyes off Will. He looked so sad as he stared at the happy youngsters. As the captain read the words, "I now pronounce you to be husband and wife together—what God has joined together, let not man put asunder," Will's black eyes looked piercingly into her own. She thought he mouthed the word "Someday," but perhaps the tears filling her own eyes had tricked her.

The captain welcomed passengers and shipmates to his cabin. The cook had baked a surprisingly good little cake. There was music and laughter.

Hannah looked, but could not find Will anywhere. Somehow he did not feel like celebrating.

Chapter 11

annah spent many of the next days trying to entertain Karla and Louisa. Though she'd not had much experience with children before, except as a servant who ran errands for her nieces and nephew, she was a natural born child-rearer. She loved the two Woodcutter girls deeply and pitied them in the loss of their sister. But most of all she yearned for them to be happy again, as they were in the early days of the voyage. They seemed contented since the day they were saved, but so quiet!

Mistress Woodcutter appeared to have pulled herself into a shell. She ate and took care of her daily needs, but it seemed she did everything in a trance.

"Will, I don't even think she sees the girls any more," Hannah said as they stood at the rail one day. "Karla tore her favorite green dress the other day on a splinter in the water keg. She came into the cabin near tears saying, 'Oh Mama, I'm sorry.' And her mother never even acknowledged that she'd been spoken to. Miz Planter mended the dress, and I let Karla cry on my shoulder. I fear for the woman's mind."

Will sighed. "'Twas the deep shock of losing little Marta

that has made her this way. Sometimes it takes another deep shock to awaken someone from this dazed state. In the meantime, Hannah, thanks be to God that you ladies are in such close quarters. Perhaps you others can stand in the gap left by the mother's state of mind for Karla and Louisa."

Hannah smiled. Always her beloved found things to thank God for. She wondered if he could be thankful were he forced to share such close quarters with six other people. But Will was right.

The Frenchman who slept in Will's cabin still seemed unable to comprehend any German. Neither had he picked up any of the English which Captain Phillip spoke to some of the sailors, as Hannah and Will had. A love for children, however, is a universal language, and he smiled from ear to ear as he presented Karla and Louisa with beautiful hand carved doll babies.

Will shrugged when Hannah turned questioning eyes to him. "I guess that must be what he's been working on all these evenings over in the corner of the room. It appears even one who could not understand anything being said around him could sense the girls' loneliness."

Captain Phillip spent as much time with Karla and Louisa as he could spare, but the storm early in their voyage had taken them far off course, and he seemed always busy checking charts and maps.

So Hannah tried desperately to entertain. Each morning when she awoke she would say to herself, "Today I will teach Louisa to knit," or "Today I will see to it that the girls each walk all the way around the deck at least five times." Hannah had never given up her old custom of planning each day's activities and setting goals. But each evening she felt a bit undone as she had to admit to herself again that, though perhaps her goals for that day had been accomplished, she still could see no happiness in the girls'

faces. *If only their mother would respond to them again*,
she thought. Often she remembered what Will had said
about how it sometimes took another deep shock to bring
such a person around. Without really thinking, she prayed
for just such a shock, then wondered with fear in her heart
if she could rescind that prayer.

They had been at sea for exactly two months when
once again the boat began to toss back and forth ferociously.
This time, however, though again the storm was violent,
they were prepared. They had noticed how red the sky was
that morning and as the wind began to increase, Captain
Phillip had yelled orders at everyone. They had battened
down everything, and the cook had quickly prepared
some food ahead so that at least they would have something to eat. And it seemed all had found their "sea legs,"
for no one became ill during this storm.
from topside, and when he could see that it was getting
from topside and when he could see that it was getting
worse, he ordered all passengers to their cabins for the
storm's duration.

"Captain," Will shouted, "you look so happy. Are you
one of those sailors who enjoys a storm?"

"No, man!" the officer yelled. "But if we have to have
us a storm, at least she is coming from the right direction.
With any luck, mayhap she will blow us right back on
course where we ought to be. Now get to your cabins,
all of ye—and be quick about it!"

Hannah and Will lingered in the corridor for a brief
moment after the rest had found their bunks.

"Darling," he whispered, "be careful during this storm.
I worried so about you that last time. And, please, stay
here in your cabin where you belong. I'd not rest at all if
I thought you were roaming the ship as you did before."

His concern for her touched her deeply. With a quick
glance in both directions to make sure all was clear, she

grabbed hold of his arm and kissed his cheek. "I'll be good. And I pray you'll be well this time, my love."

"Oh Hannah," he sighed and pulled her into his arms, kissing her soundly. Just then the rain began to lash the sails in fury, and they each ran into their respective cabins. Hannah hoped her roommates would think it was the wind which had brought the high color to her cheeks.

In the middle of the night, Hannah awoke to low moaning coming from the far bunk, occupied by Miz Planter.

"Oh no, not again. I don't know if I can face all that again," she mumbled as she tried to make her way to the lady's bunk.

Holding herself from falling into the bunk by supporting her hands against the top bed, Hannah mumbled, "Miz Planter, what is it? Are you ill?"

"No, Hannah. I—oh, help me! I think the baby is coming."

Hannah felt herself get sick with fear. "But Miz Planter, I've never even seen—I thought there was another month—oh dear! I don't have any idea what to do." Without realizing it, she had raised her voice to almost a frenzied scream.

Miz Planter groaned and Hannah sensed in the darkness that she was muffling a scream against a pillow. In a minute, she spoke again. "'Tisn't supposed to be my time yet for at least another month, but is appears no one told this youngin' that. The pains took me shortly after we came to bed. I'm sorry I woke you."

"Stuff and nonsense!" Hannah tried to laugh. "Can you tell me what to do?"

"'Tis my first child. I don't . . . oh . . . uh . . ." Again Hannah heard moanings as coming through a stuffed pillow.

Shaking with cold or fear, she knew not which, Hannah sensed the need was immediate. She stumbled uphill against the pitch of the boat and screamed, "Grandmama! Wake up! I need your help! It's Miz Planter's time!" She shouted repeatedly and shook the old lady's shoulders but she could not rouse her.

Suddenly another voice, cool and calm, came from Mistress Woodcutter's bunk. "Let her sleep, Hannah. I think you and I can handle this. But we definitely need light. Can you light the oil lamp?"

Hannah didn't question the fact that Mistress Woodcutter had at long last joined their world again. She was moving as one in a dream, trying to find the lamp when the older lady spoke again.

"No Hannah—with this rough water mayhap a lamp wouldn't be safe. You see if you can reach the lantern on the deck above the water barrel."

When she'd retrieved the lantern, Mistress Woodcutter sent her out again for a tub of water. "Should be boiled," the woman said, "but there's no time."

When Hannah returned with the water, the cabin had been transformed into a hospital. Karla sat on the bunk above Miz Planter holding the lantern out so that it swung freely. The child's eyes were wide with fear though she did not seem to be fully awake. From somewhere strips of cloth had been tied to the bedposts and Miz Planter's hands clung to these. Hannah stood near the bed holding the water, tipping the tub with each wave so as to keep it from spilling.

Suddenly Miz Planter's back arched above the mattress and she yanked on the cloth strips with all her might. Mistress Woodcutter said, "Scream if you want. No one would hear except us above this storm." But no sound escaped the woman's lips.

Between the birth pains, Mistress Woodcutter scrambled around the tilting cabin gathering the needed supplies; her scissors, a strong cord, and a clean cloth. The sleepy Karla eventually laid down and held the lantern just above the head of the bed.

Though to Hannah it seemed to be hours, it was actually only twenty-two minutes after she had been awakened that a lusty cry escaped the lips of Miz Planter's new little boy.

Mistress Woodcutter proved to be a very efficient mid-wife indeed, though in later days she was to smile hesitantly and say, "One does what one has to do." She ministered to the needs of mother and babe so competently that the mother often said, "I never even wished for a doctor. I knew I was in good hands."

For the first two days of the baby's life, he needed no rocking chair. The ship continued to rock him, sometimes violently. Word of the new birth spread through the ship's grapevine and the cook began to bring special dishes to the young mother. From the beginning the baby was strong and healthy.

Mistress Woodcutter allowed her two daughters to take almost complete charge of the wee lad. Hannah was so thankful to see smiles lighting Karla's and Louisa's faces that she didn't even worry that the baby would be spoiled. The only things the little girls could not do for him was to change him and feed him. His mother glowed with pride as he suckled against her breast.

On the third day, the cabin of seven ladies and one wee man-child awoke to a quiet ship.

Grandmama argued it would be the death of Miz Planter and the man child, but the new mother stubbornly insisted on getting up and taking her son outside. And so, bundled up in several cloaks and escorted on one side by Hannah and the other by Mistress Woodcutter, Miz Planter took her son out to meet the captain, the crew, and to see his world. The baby blinked in the bright sunlight. Everyone declared him to be a bonnie lad.

It was Will who asked the question no one else had yet asked, since their thoughts had all been of the storm.

"What's his name, Miz Planter?"

"Well, I've thought and thought on that, Mr. Stivers. His first name is Walter, after my husband. I think in full it shall be Walter Wedgewood Planter." All nodded in agreement, and Captain Phillip beamed his approval.

The middle of that same afternoon, Mother and Baby slept soundly in their bunk. George and Gretchen were playing jackstones with Karla and Louisa. Mistress Woodcutter, now back to herself, was talking with her brother-in-law. Hannah was walking hand in hand with Grandmama. Will stood at the edge of the passageway admiring the blue sky when, from high in the crow's nest, a sailor with a field glass shouted what they'd begun to believe they would never hear.

"Land Ho!"

Chapter 12

aturally the crew and the passengers were all excited. The captain took the glass and went aloft. Shortly he returned with news that indeed land had been spotted.

"We're there! We're there! Mama, we're going to see Daddy! We're finally at the new world!" Karla and Louisa shouted as they danced in each other's arms.

"Ho there, my nieces, calm yourselves," the captain instructed. "'Tis land ahead of us, true. But we cannot be quite sure it is America. And if it is America, she is a mighty big land. We cannot be sure we are at the right spot of her shore. So ye best be calm. 'Twill likely be several days— aye, mayhap even weeks afore you'll be touching your dainty little feet on dry land again."

With these sobering words, the entire ship's company became quiet again and went about their business.

By bedtime that evening one did not need a spyglass to see the land, for the winds had been favorable all day, ever blowing the *Wedgewood* nearer her goal. Just before nightfall, Hannah strolled to the bow of the ship. Far off in the distance she could make out a line of dark green just at the horizon. She blinked trying hard to see if she could bring any details of the shoreline into focus. Though she had to admit that to stand on something solid that never moved would indeed be a treat, her heart was heavy within her.

"A penny for your thoughts, My Lady."

Hannah was startled and whirled to see Will. Then her eyes registered that for all practical purposes, they were alone on the deck. She turned back to face the western horizon.

"Oh, I was just wondering what it's going to be like. From here it looks innocent enough. Just a trace of dark green below the setting sun. But I was wondering what the future holds for us in this new land." Involuntarily she shuddered.

He dared not touch her for fear some sailor might stumble on to them. But in a very low voice, he commanded, "Hannah, look at me!"

She stared up into his radiant eyes. "Please do not be afraid of what is to come. 'Tis true that we do not know all the future holds, but there are two things we do know. Number one is that we know the future holds freedom for us."

She interrupted, "Four long years away!"

"'Tis freedom all the same," he insisted. "And secondly, while we do not know what the future holds, we both know who holds that future. Always remember that. Goodnight, My Lady."

As he spoke they had turned to face west again. Hannah nodded and turned to promise Will that she would remember, but she realized he had left to go to his cabin. It had been a beautiful benediction to a long, tiring day.

The *Wedgewood* was not as far off course as Captain Woodcutter had surmised. When they got so close to shore that it looked as though you could touch the trees, he had taken a dinghy ashore to a little seaside village to get their bearings. That evening he blew the whistle four times in rapid succession. All the passengers knew that meant to assemble on deck for a briefing.

"I've called ye all here to tell ye your journey is nearly at an end," he began.

Though she smiled and clapped with the others, Hannah's heart ached within her.

"If the winds remain favorable and we've no reason to believe they won't, we shall pull into the port of Norfolk, Virginia, two days hence. Though ye may think of the New World as raw and untamed, Norfolk is already in fact a fine thriving little town. I tell ye this because ye will mayhap want to look your best. In any case, ye should be gathering together all your gear and be ready to depart the *Wedgewood* in perhaps forty-eight hours or so."

The excitement was contagious. Karla and Louisa were fairly bursting with joy. Grandmama stood with her hand on Gretchen's shoulder silently praying that God would keep them near to George.

Captain Woodcutter went on. "When we get into port it all gets frenzied and hectic as we unload the hold. So let me speak my piece to ye now." He cleared his throat and all could see that he was choking back emotion. "This has been a long and sometimes hard journey. I want to say that all of ye, even the women, have proved to be good sailors." Everyone smiled. "I am so very sorry that we lost the best little sailor of all on this voyage. I pray that my brother and sister-in-law will forgive me for this."

Mistress Woodcutter looked at him, through tears, and whispered, "No need, Phillip."

But then the captain brightened. "But thanks be, God never takes away without giving and He gave us all little Walter Wedgewood on this trip." Everyone smiled and nodded. "I was also glad to be able to unite this young

91

couple in marriage. I would've liked to marry others, but 'twas not to be." Everyone looked confused. Hannah dropped her eyes. "Well, I guess I've had my say, except I want to thank ye all for bein' a first-rate ship's company. For those of ye who're to be indentured ashore, I pray ye'll find a happy lot. To all of ye, may God bless ye." He saluted, then turned to walk away.

"Wait a minute, sir," came a call from Hannah's left. She turned to see the cook stepping forward. "Ya know that little matter I spoke of to you before. Well, I've talked it over with the lady and she's agreed. Can we do it now?"

The captain smiled. "Of course. Uh—folks, I've been piloting shiploads of indentureds to America for several years. And in all this time, this is the first time anything like this has ever happened. Ye all know Miz Planter was to be indentured for six years in the New World. It now appears that is not to be. Mister Michael here, or Cook as you know him, has purchased her freedom for her."

A stir arose among the crowd. "How could he?" some whispered.

"Well, I set a fair price for Miz Planter's service for six years. Seems Cookie's been a-hoarding his money for years, for he gave me cash on the barrel head. Howsomever, it does not seem to be his wish for Miz Planter to work for him—that is unless you count being his wife as work!"

Everyone buzzed with joy as Miz Planter, with Walter Wedgewood in her arms, was escorted to the front of the crowd by Cookie Michael. Once again Captain Phillip performed the simple ceremony uniting the two people in marriage. The new little family retired to the captain's cabin as everyone else went to their beds.

The next day was once again declared a work day. The ladies all joined in the laundry detail. Hannah wondered if this would be the last time she could serve Will. When would she get a chance to wash his clothing again?

That afternoon tub after tub of hot water was carried to the ladies' cabin. Tongues wagged and plans were made as all seven women, married and single, rich and poor, young and old together, washed their hair and bodies and packed their things.

And so it was that on the afternoon of October 26, 1752, the *Wedgewood* pulled into the port of Norfolk. Hannah had braided her hair and Gretchen had wound the braids like a coronet around Hannah's head. Will thought she had never looked lovelier than she did when she emerged into the bright sunlight carrying her valise.

Hannah's eyes could not take in, neither could her mind grasp, all the busy hubbub of the port. There were roust-abouts going to and fro on shore carrying huge crates as easily as they might lift a feather. There was a long low row of buildings off to the right where most of the strong dark-skinned men were hauling their burdens. Hannah presumed the buildings were warehouses, but had no idea what treasures they might contain.

A ship was just pulling in to their left. It was a much smaller ship than the *Wedgewood*. One needn't wonder for long what it carried, for suddenly the air was so per-meated with the smell of fish that Hannah gasped for breath. A huge net of fish had been drawn up at the corners by some type of winch, and now the fish were tumbling through an opening in the net into boxes. As soon as one box was full, another was shoved into its place. Then men carried the boxes to the warehouses, singing a chant in a minor key. Many of the fish were still alive, for they flipped and flopped around. Occasionally, one would flip out of a box. The carriers seemed not to notice, and no sooner would one flip out than any of a number of small Negroes would run and pick it up. Hannah took special note of one child. He could be no more than eight years old. He had grabbed two of the fallen fishes before the other children reached them. Now he shouted gleefully, "Got Missy's dinner!" Silently, Hannah wondered who Missy was.

From the other side of the ship an awful commotion arose. With the other passengers, Hannah ran through the passageway between the men's and ladies' quarters to see what could be seen. There was the sharp crack of a whip followed by a piercing scream. Hannah recoiled in horror as she saw what was taking place on the neighboring ship's deck. About 20 black people, all stark naked, stood chained together at both their wrists and their ankles. There was a tiny, weasel-eyed man, laying a bull whip expertly across the back of the first man in the line. Hannah felt faint, yet the scene would not disappear even when she closed her eyes.

"Wh-why d-doesn't he m-move? That seems t-to b-be wh-what that m-man with the wh-whip wants," said the pimply-faced sailor just behind her.

"I don't think he understands," Hannah whispered.

Thankfully, just then the *Wedgewood* ship's company began to descend their own gangplank and attention was diverted from the goings-on aboard the slave ship.

Hannah hugged Miz Planter-Michael as she and Cookie proudly walked over the walkway. Cookie would hopefully find a position at a fine restaurant here in Norfolk and together with Walter Wedgewood they would live a fairy-tale life.

Mistress Woodcutter, Karla, and Louisa were the next to depart. A man who could have been the captain's twin had appeared driving a covered carriage. The girls had flown down the gangplank screaming "Papa!" Hannah turned away from the scene when she heard the man ask, "But where is Marta?"

Just then Captain Woodcutter had called all the "indentureds" to the rear of the ship. "I'll do my best," he assured them as he led them away from the general clamor on shore to a large tree stump.

Will never let go of Hannah's hand as the sale progressed. First the youngest boy was sold to a blacksmith who seemed an amiable fellow. Then the Frenchman went to a stern-looking well-dressed man whom the captain said was a banker. Next, the captain called Grandmama, Gretchen, and George to step up on the tree stump.

"Now, here I have for ye a wonderful bargain, folks. These young people have just recently wed. The old lady here is her grandmother. Seems old, but quite spry I can tell ye. Only problem is hearing. Now they all are for sale for a six-year period. What will ye bid?"

Evidently George had agreed to work two years longer to stay with Gretchen, Hannah decided.

"Don't want the women. Give you $250 for the boy," someone shouted.

Will squeezed Hannah's hand so hard her fingers ached. "Please God," she whispered.

"Come now folks. Ye can do better than that. Some of ye cotton plantation owners—George here would make a fine overseer. Gretchen is a hard worker. She'd make yer lady a fine maid. The old lady can cook. What am I bid?"

"$450 for the young couple. Don't want the old woman. Just have to bury her."

The captain shook his head solemnly. "Ye can do better than that! Does anyone want all three?"

The three on the stump plead with the crowd with their eyes. Will and Hannah prayed.

"I'll go $450 for all three of them," a great red-faced man shouted.

"Sold," said the captain with a sigh.

"Bless him," Hannah choked. "Oh Will, it could have been us!" she whispered.

Will had realized the same thing simultaneously and he too was choked with emotion. "Mayhap there is still hope," he responded.

The captain called their names. "This is Will and Hannah. They also wish to be sold together." Evidently he could not make himself lie for them. "They will work for four years. What am I bid?"

"That's the one I've been waiting to bid on. The man I represent down in Carolina wants a strong man to work his cotton. I'll give you $800 right now for him."

"But what of Hannah?" the captain implored.

"Don't want the wench," the big man guffawed. "Let someone else buy her. All I's supposed to bring home is a strong-looking buck."

The captain cleared his throat. "As I said before I'd rather keep these two together. Are there other bidders?"

The silence was deafening to Hannah. It seemed they had been on the stump for hours with no one saying a word. She felt like an animal that all eyes were inspecting. Never had Hannah imagined the horror of looking into all those eyes. Even the women in the crowd seemed to view her as nothing more than a piece of property to be bid upon. Finally, from the rear of the crowd a familiar voice spoke.

"Phillip, Mark says I can purchase Hannah's services to help me with the girls for the next four years." Hannah couldn't believe her ears, for 'twas her friend, Mistress Woodcutter, who spoke. "I'll pay $300 for her."

"But what of Will?" the captain implored.

His brother spoke back in a gruff tone. "Can't afford the both. Don't need a man just now. In truth, we don't *need* the girl, but I told her she could . . ." The voice trailed off.

"C'mon captain," shouted the Carolinian. "$800 cash for—what did you call him? Will? Take it or leave it."

"I'm sorry, Stivers. I tried," Phillip Woodcutter mumbled

under his breath. "Sold!" he shouted.

As the purchasers met the captain to make good on their bids, Will pulled Hannah away from the crowd. She tried hard to be brave, but tears filled her eyes.

"If only," she began.

He gently placed his hand against her lips. "No time for if only's, my lady. In four years we will be free. Do you see that lovely church spire pointing toward God's heaven on yonder corner?"

In truth, Hannah had not seen the church. The horrors of the dock area were all she could see. Far off, down the shore, the negroes from the slave ship were being sold. Everywhere, all Hannah could see seemed filthy and sweaty and dirty and vile. Just a few feet toward the ship were two men who were lying in their own vomit, so drunk were they. Hannah had never been so repulsed as she was by this so-called wonderful land of America. But now Will was lifting her chin with his hand.

"My lady, please! There is no time! Do you see the church?"

Hannah nodded mutely. It looked as though over there, several hundred yards from all the dirt and stench of the dock area, were the beginnings of a lovely residential area. A white wooden church with a large steeple stood on the corner.

Will spoke again. "Let that be our meeting place. Wherever we are, after the four years, we shall both return to that church. Whoever arrives first shall attend every service until the other one comes. Will you wait for me here if you arrive first?"

Her body shook with sobs, but she nodded. "You know I shall."

Suddenly he drew her to himself in an embrace that nearly stifled her. "I love you, My Lady."

"Stivers, it's time to go," the captain called. Will picked

up his valise, kissed Hannah's forehead, and said, "In four years—at the church!"

Hannah hurried to where the Woodcutter's carriage stood waiting for her. During her last few moments with Will, Karla had placed her valise in the trunk of the carriage.

"C'mon Hannah," Louisa called.

With tears streaming and head down, Hannah accepted Mark Woodcutter's help climbing aboard. Suddenly the air was split by a shout from a wagon heading south.

"Hannah!"

She turned and wiped the tears from her eyes just in time to see Will standing and waving beautiful white woolen mittens at her.

She lifted her arm in a return farewell, and then the buckboard in which Will rode turned out of sight.

"Let's go home, Mr. Woodcutter," her new mistress said.

Part 3

Indentured

Chapter 13

he carriage bounced over the cobblestone streets, and before long the road turned to dirt. Trees nearly closed in on them, but the cool of the shade was refreshing. For a fall day, it was very hot. As they rode along, the inside of the carriage turned first red, then orange, and sometimes a bright golden, reflecting the surrounding scenery.

"Oh Mama, aren't the trees beautiful? God is certainly painting a beautiful landscape for us," Louisa said.

Mr. Woodcutter fairly exploded from his driver's seat. The front window of the carriage was open and he'd been listening to his daughter. "I'll have no more mention of God, child!" he shouted. "There cannot be a God in heaven—else I'd be driving a carriage full of three daughters instead of just two!"

"But, Papa—I . . . " Louisa began.

"And don't sass me girl! Your baby sister wouldn't *ever* have sassed me. We are no longer Christians in our house. God has left me comfortless, if there even is a God!"

Louisa was wide-eyed with fear but brokenhearted and confused at the same time. How could her Papa whom she idolized have become this burly oaf whom she hardly knew?

Hannah put her arm around Louisa as the tiny girl sobbed quietly against her shoulder. Karla sat dry-eyed but trembling all over. Mistress Woodcutter buried her face in her hands and whispered, "'Tis exactly the reaction I feared."

"What? Speak up back there or don't speak at all!" shouted the hateful Mr. Mark.

All was quiet for several minutes. Hannah noticed that the air no longer seemed tinged with gold or red. She thought perhaps the sun had gone behind clouds, until the fragrance of pine so permeated the coach that she realized they were in a lovely evergreen forest. On and on they rode in silence, the tension in the coach so heavy it seemed to suffocate all life and joy.

"Well, here we are," said Mr. Mark and he reined in the horses. "Home, such as it is! But it will surely be quiet without my little Marta." The speaker's voice broke and he jumped to the ground and ran off, disappearing into the woods.

The ladies slowly disembarked from the high carriage, Hannah immediately assuming her place as servant and helping the others. They stood thus, huddled together in the midst of a beautiful clearing before a lovely stone house, their first view of home in the New World.

The entire structure was two stories high. A porch ran the length of the house, its roof supported by great pillars, painted green to match the surrounding pine trees.

"Oh Mama, it's beautiful," whispered Karla.

Hannah thought she had never seen anything so grand! The Woodcutters must be rich folk, indeed.

"I told him I would live in a log house. But he wouldn't have it! Said he was going to present me with a castle in the New World!" the mistress said bitterly. "I wanted to come with him, or at least a year ago . . . but no! I had to wait till he'd hauled all this stone out here in the middle of nowhere and then finished this house."

Mistress Woodcutter stood staring at the magnificent home in the pines, seemingly to have forgotten about the girls and Hannah as she rambled along to herself.

"Well, mayhap we should go inside. Mr. Mark mayn't be back before full dark, so full of grief is he. Shall we?" Hannah said with a forced cheerfulness as she picked up their bags.

Just then the front door of the mansion opened and an old Negro man came running toward them.

"Lawsy me. They's here, Mantha! Oh Lawd have mercy, ladies come inside. Where be Mister Mark?" he sang in the most melodic voice Hannah had ever heard. Even though English was still a strange language to her, she could understand that this sweet old gray-haired black man truly was concerned that his new mistress had been given such a poor introduction to her new home. "Manthy!" he called again.

Just then the door slammed again and Hannah was witness to a great reunion. "Samantha!" shouted Karla and Louisa in unison as they ran into the ample arms of the Negro lady who stood on the porch, red turban hiding her gray hair.

The slave turned questioning eyes toward the mistress after loving the girls and exclaiming over how they'd grown in the two years since she'd come to America with "Mista Mark."

It seemed all the pent-up emotions in Hannah's new mistress just gave way as if someone had opened the floodgates of a dam. "Oh, Samantha, we lost little Marta at sea. And Mark—it's like he's gone mad. He ran off in the woods," she sobbed into the great lady's shoulder.

Immediately, this one called Samantha took charge. "Leroy, you get the bags and care for the horse. The rest of you all come inside. I's been trying to keep a dinner warm for nigh onto an hour. Celia will draw you some water to get the carriage dust off'n you afore you sit down."

As she spoke, they had entered the foyer. It seemed to Hannah to be a castle out of a fairy land. Hannah would later discover that this mansion was built much along the lines of the neighboring plantation homes. The doorway opened into a wide hall which ran from the front porch straight through the house to the back porch. The open, highly-carved balustrade followed the curved stairway up to the second floor just to the right of the huge front double door. To the left of the hallway and running the full depth of the house was a magnificent dining room. Across the hall and similar in size was a huge drawing room. While everything in the dining room was done in hand-polished mahogany accented with red velvet and gold, the drawing room was light and airy and seemed almost to blend into the outdoors. The entire south wall was windows, where curtains remained fully open much of the time. The furnishings in this room were in light greens and blues and the woodworkings of a very pale oak. Out back and connected by a small door to the dining room was an open-air sort of kitchen. The rooms where the three slaves lived were tidy little cubicles attached to the shelter house kitchen. They fairly glowed from their twice yearly whitewashing.

Upstairs, one turned to the right in the hallway and found identical rooms on the left and right. The left one was furnished for the girls, while across the hall was a nursery fully-equipped with toys, desks, and a white steel-framed bedstead for the governess. At the opposite end of the hall was the master bedroom across from what would have been Marta's room, empty now and untouched for many months to come. Every room in the mansion could boast its own fireplace; the dining and drawing rooms each had two. Great care had been used in selecting furnishings. The house had more closet space than one could imagine. It was in every way a dream house, but for tonight all that could truly interest the weary travelers was food, cleanliness, and sleep.

Mistress Woodcutter and the girls were being bustled off up the great stairway by the maid, referred to as Celia. Hannah found herself face to face with the cook. Thankfully, at the top of the stairs, Mistress Woodcutter remembered to introduce her.

"Oh Samantha, this is Hannah. She's to be the girls' . . . uh . . . governess, I guess. She'll be with us for the next four years."

As soon as the mistress was out of sight, Samantha turned hate-filled eyes on Hannah.

"Governess—eh? Just a fancy name for a white house-slave, I reckon."

"Oh no, uh . . . Samantha. I'm not a slave. I'm an indentured servant."

"Oh—a *charity* case. How'd you get her to feel sorry for you? Well, follow me. You can have the little room at the . . ."

The hateful cook was interrupted by a call from upstairs. It must be Celia, as Hannah had not yet heard her speak.

"Manthy, the lady wants that 'ere Hannah's bags up here in the nursery!"

"Hotsy totsy!" Samantha grumbled. "Guess you'll be sleeping upstairs like you was somebody special!"

As she trudged up the long stairs, the weary Hannah sighed. *Will I have to deal with her for four long years?*

Chapter 14

annah didn't realize how tired she was until her trembling body fell into bed several hours later. Could it really have been less than twenty-four hours ago that she had disembarked from the *Wedgewood*, hand in hand with her darling, Will? Her emotions had risen to high hopes and been dashed to despair so many times in one day that it seemed weeks had passed. She was truly grateful for her new-found station in life. Mistress Woodcutter had proven to be a wonderful friend, to help her out by paying her fare in return for four years of teaching the sweet Karla and lovely Louisa. But establishing herself in this household was going to be a challenge.

Mistress had already laid out a few guidelines. After they'd each bathed the road dust away, the mighty Samantha had bellowed from the foot of the steps, "I said your dinner is awaiting!"

Hannah poked her head out the door of the nursery as she heard the family passing. Mistress must have sensed the question in her mind.

"Come now, Hannah. You are to take all your meals with the family. My dear, we want you not to think of yourself as a servant but as a part of our family." With this, she linked her arm through Hannah's and they descended the stairs together.

Samantha was bustling around filling plates from the sideboard as they entered. She glared at Hannah and said, "The kitchen is through . . ." but the mistress interrupted.

"Mantha," she spoke slowly. "Hannah is to eat with the girls and me. Not just tonight, but every meal. You and Celia and Leroy are to treat her with the same respect you do me, for she is a new member of our family. Do you understand?"

The big black lady nodded. "Yes, missy. I understands," she smiled at the mistress. But Hannah heard the bitterness in her voice as she shouted, "Celia, bring back the plate I done tol' you to remove. The new governess will be a-needin' it."

Hannah's senses seemed to be reeling as she sat at the table. It was too much to take in at once. The silver candelabra in the center of the table gleamed; the fine crystal water glasses sparkled in the candlelight. And the aroma of the mums in the centerpiece mingled with the smell of ham, candied yams, fresh corn, and fantastic bread.

Mistress Woodcutter told the girls to mind their manners and slow down as they ate. But even she and Hannah nearly gobbled the food, 'twas so wonderful after their meals on the *Wedgewood*. When Hannah had eaten her fill and was beginning to relax, Celia entered from the kitchen with a three layer chocolate cake in one hand and a deep dish apple pie in the other.

"Oh Mommy, can I have a piece of each?" Karla begged just as Samantha appeared to cut the dessert.

The cook beamed from ear to ear and was already placing a portion of each dessert on one plate when Mistress Woodcutter addressed Hannah.

"Mantha's desserts are not to be believed, Hannah. She

106

will certainly put some meat on these bones. But what do you think, Hannah? Hasn't Karla already had an awfully lot to eat?"

Hannah flushed as she realized that she had already been elevated to the position of governess, for she was being asked her opinion. She weighed the matter carefully before she responded.

"Well, I can see that both desserts are very enticing," she smiled at Samantha. "But mayhap, 'twould be better if the child did not overload her tummy as it has been so long since we've tasted such a rich meal."

Karla's face clouded and Samantha moved behind the mistress, shooting dagger looks at the intruder.

"My thinking exactly, Hannah," responded Mistress Woodcutter. "Give us each a piece of your pie now, Mantha, and save the cake for our lunch tomorrow."

Karla was immediately appeased, but Hannah knew she'd made an enemy of the big Negro slave.

After the delicious meal was completed, Celia carried pail after pail of heated water up the stairs to matching copper tubs which had been placed in the end of the long nursery. Thus began a bedtime ritual which Hannah imagined would be repeated many times during the four long years she would serve the Woodcutters. While the girls disrobed, Hannah hunted through their valises till she found clean gowns for them. The gowns smelled sweet and clean from that washday two days ago on board ship. Hannah's eyes filled with tears as she remembered washing Will's clothing. But she could not go deeper in her reverie for from across the hall she heard—

"He will too!"

"Will not!"

"Will too!"

"Karla! Louisa! What is all the hubbub?" asked the new governess as she entered the room.

107

Both girls were seated in the steaming tubs trying to make suds from the stubborn lye soap.

"Karla said Papa won't come back to our lovely new house. Not tonight, and maybe not ever. She said he hates us and that he wishes it was us who—" Louisa's voice broke and her eyes filled with tears.

"Oh girls, you mustn't think such thoughts. Your papa is heartsick and can probably scarce believe that Marta is gone. Remember how we felt when it first happened?" As she spoke, Hannah was scrubbing Louisa's back vigorously. She picked up the kettle and poured water down her back. "There now—you finish yourself while I help Karla get the soap off her back," she instructed.

As the girls rubbed themselves with thick thirsty towels and slipped into the flannel gowns, Hannah went on.

"It may take your papa a great deal of time to work through his hurt and sadness. He may be very hard for you to understand. But girls, we must never lose hope. And we shall pray that God will ease his hurt. We must always be kind to him and patiently wait on God to answer our prayers."

Leroy had started a fire in the nursery hearth during the dinner hour. Now both girls sat on a lovely thick rug in front of the fire as Hannah tenderly cared for their long blonde hair. First she unbraided it, then she took the brush and brushed through their hair again and again till it shone.

"But, why doesn't he like us anymore, Hannah? 'Tisn't our fault about Marta," declared the younger girl sadly.

"Aach! Darlings, your papa still loves you. Don't think for even a moment that he doesn't. 'Tis only his heartache that keeps him from showing it now. There, I think you are presentable to go give your mother a goodnight kiss and hug."

She had rebraided their long blonde hair into one long braid down each back to keep it from tangling as they slept. She thought they looked like angels as they departed to find their mother.

Soon the girls were back, each holding one of Mistress Woodcutter's hands, as they said in unison, "Goodnight, Hannah."

The mistress looked so tired and sad. "Hannah, thank you for caring for their baths. I find I am weary to the bone, but I also want to spend a few minutes with these angels tonight. Normally bedtime routine shall be yours alone to care for, but tonight I shall read them a story. I've instructed Celia to bring you fresh hot water if you care to bathe."

"Thank you, Ma'am. Goodnight girls." As they turned to go, Hannah whispered, "Mistress, has the Master returned?"

"No. Goodnight Hannah," she mumbled as she followed the girls across the hall to their room.

Celia had silently cared for emptying the girls' tubs. She smiled at Hannah, and Hannah supposed she should try to befriend the girl, but she was too tired tonight to care. Hannah did mumble, "Thanks," as the girl prepared another tub of steaming water for her.

And now she was in this wonderful soft bed amid sweet-smelling sheets, so different from her top bunk on the *Wedgewood*. True to her promise, Hannah prayed for God's grace to be sufficient to help her new master in this hour. And then of course, she prayed for Will. She wondered where he was and if his new master was being kind to him. A tear trickled down her cheek. She fell into an exhausted sleep with the memory of him standing, waving the white woolen mittens from the departing wagon.

For a moment Hannah could not remember where she was or why. She only knew that it was pitch dark. What had awakened her? She sat upright and listened carefully.

It was the voice of her mistress. Even though it drifted the entire length of the enormous hallway, it was raised to such a pitch that Hannah readily understood every word.

"Oh Mark, please don't say such a thing. 'Twas nothing I could do. She was always a frail little thing. The illness was just too much for her. Mark, look at me. It wasn't my fault. What are you doing?"

The master's voice boomed. His speech had slurred enough that Hannah knew he had been into alcohol. "I'm moving my stuff to the shed, that's what. If you think I'm gon' sleep wif the murderer of my darlin' Marta, you're crazed!"

"Mark, how can you think that I am to blame? I nursed her day and night. Please Mark, don't do this! What will I tell the girls?"

"Tell them anything you want," he shouted. Hannah prayed they hadn't woken up to hear this as she had. "They're alive, like you are. And 'tisn't fair!"

The mistress spoke again, audibly trying to calm herself. "Mark, don't go away. I need you. I miss her too." Her voice broke and she choked out, "We must remember 'The Lord giveth and the Lord taketh' . . ."

Hannah shuddered as she heard the awful sound of a slap. Mark bellowed, "Don't ever speak to me of God again! There canna' be a God if my baby is dead."

Now the mistress' voice was raised to a frenzied pitch. "All right, then—go to your shed or wherever you want. If truth were known, 'tis your fault she had to die."

"My fault? I wasn't even on the ship! How could it possibly be—?"

"Yes, you were not on the ship! You were not anywhere for the past two long years. I needed you so many times. I wanted to come with you to America so badly. I would've lived in a cave or a tent to be with you. But no! You had to come here and build me this mansion

110

before you would have the girls and I come. Mayhap if we would have done it my way—oh Mark!"

The slamming of the door and footfalls down the stairway were followed by long moaning sobs.

Hannah longed to go to her mistress and try to help in some way, but she must remember the hour of the night. She wouldn't want her to think she had purposely eavesdropped. She prayed long and hard that God would help the Woodcutters to pull together instead of apart in this hour of their greatest need.

'Twas beginning to lighten in the east before Hannah fell asleep again.

Chapter 15

ill was beginning to wonder if they would ever reach their destination. They had ridden in the rickety old wagon from first light until it was too dark to see for four—or was it five—days straight now. In the beginning, he had tried to memorize each landmark along the way, thinking to reverse them in four years on his return trip to Hannah. But he soon realized that task to be impossible. They rode mile after mile in silence through what appeared to be virgin forest. The wagon rose and fell over the beautiful rolling hills. The country reminded him of Germany, and Will was mentally back walking over those hills with Hannah when his companion finally spoke.

"Well, Stivers, if all goes well, we should be home tomorrow by this time of day. You're sure a quiet one, ain't ya?"

Will smiled. "'Twas wool-gatherin' again." For the first time he allowed his mind to leave Hannah to wonder what these next four years held for him. "Uh—what is 'home' to be like?" he stammered.

"'Tis a big—no, 'tis a *huge* cotton plantation."

"Does it have a name?"

"Folks about calls it 'Devon's Demonland!'"

Will shuddered.

"But you better never let Mr. Devon hear you calling it that. He sometimes gets fancy and calls it 'Devonshire,' but mostly we that work there just calls it home."

"What's it like?"

"Beautiful—if you like cotton!" Will thought he caught a note of sarcasm in the voice, but he wasn't sure.

"There are nigh onto 500 acres of uninterrupted fields of the white. Scarcely a tree on the whole place."

"And the house?" Stivers asked. "What's it like?" He remembered the beautiful castle in Germany.

"Doubt you'll ever see the inside of the big house, man. The field hands live in the quarters. They ain't much. About eight feet by ten feet with one window. You'll probably have a hut of your own, bein's that you're white.

"Do you know what my job will be, Hank?"

"All I does is buy 'em, Stivers. I'll let Devon tell you what your job is. But I'll give you some advice. No matter what he tells you to do, don't argue."

Will thought he saw the big blond-haired man at his side shudder a little. Again they fell into a comfortable silence and did not speak till they stopped to eat supper.

"Is Mr. Devon married, Hank?" Will asked.

"No, thanks be to the Almighty. For he's meaner than a treed possum when he gets some corn whiskey in him. Iff'n he had a wife, it's hard to tell what he'd do to her when he's drunk."

"Sounds like you don't like him too well," Will remarked. Hank thought for a long silent moment before answering.

"I hate every hair on Devon's ugly head!"

"Then why do you work for him?" Will asked.

"Same reason you will do whatever he wants of you for the next four years. He paid my fare on the ship. I have

113

one more year to go before I walk away from Demonland forever."

"Has it been awful then?" Will asked the obvious.

"When Devon says 'Jump' you better say 'Yes sir!' and 'How high, sir?' and 'Is it okay for me to come back down, sir?'" Both men laughed at the crude joke.

They busied themselves bedding down for the night. The two men had developed a pattern of sorts. Hank cared for the horses while Will tried to arrange leaves, branches, and whatever was near to place their bedrolls upon. They quietly ate beef jerky from the provisions Hank had brought along and then fell asleep almost instantly, exhausted from the arduous trip.

"Are you married, Hank?" Will asked the next day. Somehow the closer they came to the plantation the more important it seemed to Will to become a friend to this man.

"No. Me, I never met a woman I couldn't live without, so I never felt the need. What about you? Got a wife back in the homeland?"

"No, but in four years I will have one here," Will smiled.

"That girl they put on the stump beside you? Somehow I figured she was your sister. What was her name?" Hank asked as he slapped a pesky mosquito on his arm.

"Hannah," Will said reverently. "I love her with all my heart."

Soon Hank said, "Well—there it is, Stivers! Home to you for the next four years. Welcome to Devonshire." The sarcasm was back in his voice.

Will sat spellbound as he stared at the great flat plain which lay before him. As Hank had predicted, there were scarcely any trees, except those which lined either side of the half circle carriage drive leading to the front of the big plantation house. Hank did not take the beautiful lane, but whipped the old horse into a lather as they drove round behind the big house. A bare piece of ground separated the house from what Will presumed to be "the quarters" Hank had referred to. Will was still trying to catch his breath from the jostling ride down the hill and around the house when he heard a man shout from behind them.

"Hey there, Hank! It's about time you got home. What took you so long this trip?"

The speaker was not a large man. Will guessed him to be about forty-five years old from the gray hair round his temples. He was dressed all in white, from the top of his hat down to his pants, which were tucked into beautiful shining black riding boots. He was astride the most magnificent piece of horseflesh Will had seen in a long time, a cream-colored mare. "So Hank," he continued, "is this the best you could do?"

Will was startled at the reply. "Oh, Mr. Devon sir, I's sorry to be late. 'Tweren't no ships come into Norfolk for several days." Will stared open-mouthed at the man who fifteen minutes ago had been a confident person, now reduced to an apologetic whiner in the presence of the little man on the horse. Hank continued, "And yes, sir, Mr. Devon—he was the best I could do. He was the only single man aboard who looked even halfway strong. I only had to give $800 for him for four years. 'I's got your other $200 right here, Mr. Devon." He ran to the little man on the horse and gave him a purse.

"Well, does he speak English?" the owner inquired.

By now, Will had tired of being spoken about the way one would a piece of furniture or an animal. He stood to his feet and in his best English said, "Mr. Devon, I am Will Stivers, your humble servant, for the next four years."

"Not humble enough, I dare say," the little man replied. "Take him to the second hut, Hank. Liza will bring his supper. Stivers, did you say? I'll see you tomorrow. Sleep well. You'll need all your strength," he laughed wickedly as he rode out of sight.

Will could not believe the squalor in the quarters. Naked Negro children sat playing in the mud. From the odor it was obvious that there were no outhouses about. Hank took him into a filthy hut, shaking his head sadly.

"Welcome home," he said, choking on the dust that flew from the mattress he had patted.

As Will's eyes adjusted to the dimness, he realized that on one wall of the small hut there was a shelf holding a cornhusk tick, evidently his new bed. Toward the rear, near the only window, was a crude bench of sorts. The floor had not seen a broom in a long time and there was nothing to make this seem like a real home, not even a door.

"Land o' Goshen, it's worse than I had ever imagined," Hank mumbled. "Will, I hate to leave you here in this . . . this . . ." his hand swept the air for emphasis as he spoke. "But Mr. Devon will have my hide if I'm not in my room afore sundown. Him and Cletus, the overseer, keep an eye on all of us, slaves and indentureds alike."

"Don't worry, Hank," Will responded. "I'll be alright. Mayhap I shall see you in the morn."

"Doubt it. I don't get out here much. He keeps me busy in the house. Good luck, man." He walked to the doorway. "Oh, your neighbors there are from the islands. They don't speak any English."

Will felt totally isolated and filled with dread as Hank left the dusty yard for the big house. A skinny little mulatto girl stared at him from the door of the next hut. She wore a shift obviously made from a flour sack. Her hair, which lacked the tight curls of a true Negro, hung in greasy clumps.

"Hello," Will said softly, hoping not to frighten her. "My name is Will. Do you have a broom I may borrow?"

"No she don't—and she don't speak no English, Germ!"

came from behind him.

He turned to stare up, open-mouthed at the biggest blackest female he had ever seen. She was considerably taller than he and he guessed her weight to be at least twice his own. Her skin was as black as coal. She wore long earrings that looked like some sort of animal teeth. Her dress and turban were bright green with yellow circles. When she smiled her face lit up, highlighted by a gold-capped front tooth.

"I's Liza, German. Welcome to Devon's Demonland. I brung you some vittles. Best eat while they's hot. Gotta keep your strength up."

"Thank you," Will mumbled as he sat down in the dirt to eat. He bowed his head for a second, then engaged Liza in conversation as he devoured the food.

"It's good. Did you cook it?"

She grinned again and the tooth gleamed. "Yes. I's the best cook in all of Carolina some say."

"How long have you been here, Miss Liza?"

She laughed. "Just Liza, Germ. I don't deserve no 'Miss.' And I's lived here long as I can remember. Is you done already?"

"Yes, but can you answer a question before you go? I'm not used to such—such dirt! Is there no way I can clean my hut afore I try to sleep?"

"No brooms allowed in the quarters, Germ. You can get a bucket of water from the well in the mornin'. Can't go now causen it's too late and Cletus, he's out patrollin'. Get youself shot iff'n you out late. I gots to get back myself. G'night Germ." She picked up the old wooden bowl and ran to the house shouting as she ran, "I's got permission to be out! I's got permission!"

Will had not noticed the failing light. But after Liza left, he figured he may as well turn his attention to the home which had been assigned him. Inside it was so dark he could not see anything.

Finally he knelt near the board bed and tried to pray. Tears of fear and anger and longing for Hannah began to choke him. "Oh God," he finally stammered, "thank You that my darling is not with me. I thought my heart would break as we stood on that stump those days ago and I realized that we were really going to be separated. And all the way here I argued with You that we had done nothing to deserve the heartbreak of isolation for four long years. But now, Father, I see why it must be. Thank You for protecting her from this awful place. Thank You for letting me know she is safe at the Woodcutters." He paused for a long time trying to frame the right words for the rest of his prayer. "Oh God," he finally continued, "please help me to be able to endure whatever I must in these future months and years. And God, let me be a light for You in this dark—this utterly dark—place."

Having thus spoken he picked up the corn tick and took it to the door of the hut. There he shook it violently. Using his valise as a pillow, he made up a bed of sorts and fell into an exhausted sleep.

The trip had tired him so that the sun was shining brightly the next day before the bellow of Master Devon awoke him.

"Stivers! Will Stivers! Get out here!"

Chapter 16

any weeks had passed since that first night in the Woodcutter house. Though Hannah had found a measure of peace for herself from deep within, the home in which she lived was certainly not a happy one. Hannah had only encountered Mister Mark a few times. On each occasion he had totally ignored her—as if she did not exist. This did not bother her as much as his identical treatment of his daughters. It had become Hannah's daily duty to try to encourage their sad little hearts. The task grew to be nearly impossible.

The mistress, on the other hand, had built a wall around her emotions. No one would know from her but that everything was as it should be in this house. She forced a gaity upon all who crossed her path. Hannah knew she was trying to hide the situation from the servants, but felt certain that Samantha, Celia, and Leroy all knew their master was sleeping in the shed. Every evening the mistress made up a new excuse for Mister Mark's absence at the evening meal.

"He has business in town," or "One of the horses is ailing and he wishes to stay with it." The excuses grew more lame as the days turned into weeks. Eventually the mistress just said, "No, not tonight!" to Samantha's inevitable question as to how to set the table.

Hannah had established a good routine for the girls. Each morning she taught them the basic concepts of mathematics. They repeated tables of multiplication and division, and worked out story problems. Mister Mark had purchased learning books for his daughters before their arrival. Together Hannah, Karla, and Louisa worked at learning the English language and penmanship. After a light luncheon each day, Hannah had the tedious job of teaching them to knit. Karla was doing beautifully and had completed the back of a sweater for her papa. Louisa, however, was clumsy. She spent as much time unraveling her work back to a dropped stitch as she did in forward progress on the garment. Louisa was always eager for the hour assigned to knitting to pass so that she could escape to the great outdoors. Hannah insisted that the girls spend the larger part of the afternoon playing. Whenever weather permitted, they romped outdoors.

It had been one of the rare times when the girls had forgotten for a moment the sad condition of their home life. Hannah had been on the porch mending a tear in her stocking. She sat with a smile on her face, listening to the girls singing as they gathered wildflowers on the edge of the woods. The smile on Hannah's face froze, though, as she overheard.

"Papa! Papa! Look at the lovely flowers Karla and I have picked. Aren't they beautiful?"

"Leave me alone, child!"

Now it was the older girl who spoke, calmly but with the steel of determination in her voice.

"Papa, Louisa and I are glad to see you. We miss you. There are things we'd like to tell you. Why don't you ever come—?"

120

"It's none of your business, girl. As I told your sister, just leave me alone!"

Hannah was amazed, for Karla was usually so timid. But today she was persistent. Evidently this was a speech she had rehearsed in her mind several times.

"Papa, please hear me out. I can accept that you do not love Louisa and me anymore since Marta's—death. But as our father, there are things that we need to discuss with you. Such as—it is already the month of December. And no preparations have been made. What do you think we should get Mama for Christmas?"

"Christmas!" he bellowed. "There is to be no celebration of Christmas in this house. Not now! Not ever! Without my darling little Marta, there cannot ever be—" His voice broke.

But Karla was undaunted. Hannah wondered where she ever got the courage to go on as she did. In a perfectly controlled voice she said, "Papa, you are not the man I remember in the old country. I cannot believe you are being so selfish in your grief. All of us miss little Marta. We all loved her as much as you. But it is not my fault— nor Louisa's—that she died. And it is not our Mama's either. If you would just come home—"

The speech was never completed. Hannah heard the slap from her post on the porch. The father screamed in a beast-like tone, "Get out of my sight, both of you!" Looking back, Hannah realized that it had probably been that very night that Karla and Louisa had begun to formulate their plan.

For such youngsters, they had forgotten nothing. They had taken food. They had gathered the necessary blankets and towels and warm clothing. As Christmas day dawned, Hannah found their beds empty. At first, she thought perhaps they had gone to awaken their mother. But when they were not there, Hannah began to be alarmed. A

121

thorough search of the house and grounds was made. The girls were nowhere!

Mistress Woodcutter voiced a fear Hannah had thought too horrid for words. "Mayhap Mark has stolen them away—yes, kidnapped them—as punishment to me for allowing them to have the Christmas tree."

"Oh no, Mistress," Hannah reassured. "I am a very light sleeper. I would have heard if any had come down the hall in the night." But she asked Leroy to go to the master's shed to be sure he was there.

Leroy was back soon, shaking his head. "The master . . . he . . . uh, well . . . he sleeping crossaways on his old cot. He not even move when I shake him. He had . . . uh . . . been sick on de floor of de shed. There be . . . uh . . . well, they's a jug of corn squeezed whiskey aside him there on de floor. The jug—she be empty." He rolled his big eyes sadly. "But Hannah, I found dis here paper pinned on de door."

The note was in Karla's well-formed penmanship. "Dear Papa," it read. "Louisa and I have decided to leave this place. It is beautiful but it does not feel like home because you are never in the house with Mama and us. Since the day in the woods, we know you hate us. So now that we are gone, mayhap you and Mama can be together again and find happiness. We love you both and cannot stand seeing you like this. Mama cries every night. Louisa and I know because we sneak down to her door and listen. So please, Papa—now that you won't have to see us and always be reminded of Marta, go to our Mama and love her again." It was signed "Respectfully, Karla." Below this in Louisa's more childlike hand, it said, "Tell Mama we are sorry. We loved Marta, too. Don't hunt for us. Love, Louisa."

All the reserve the mistress had fortified herself with collapsed. Halfway through Hannah's reading of the note, she screamed and blanched white. Crying and rocking back and forth, she wrung her hands as Hannah completed the reading. Then she slumped over in a faint. She would have fallen to the floor had Leroy not caught her as she collapsed.

"This sho' be a sad day in Mister Mark's mansion house," he sing-songed.

Not knowing what else to do, Hannah took charge of the situation.

"Can you carry her up to bed, Leroy?" she implored. The old slave immediately obeyed.

"Samantha!" Hannah shouted.

The big woman lumbered in from the kitchen. "What do *you* want?" she glared.

"The mistress is sick. Leroy is taking her up to bed. She'll need cold cloths for her head and smelling salts and—"

"I guess I knows how to care for a sick woman, you little snit! Who do you think you are ordering me? Why, you're just—"

"Oh Samantha, please!" Hannah interrupted. "There isn't time for this. She has fainted dead away."

"I don't has to obey you," the slave went on. "The girls—they's your responsibility. The house—it's mine! You's not no better than me. I can do—"

"Samantha, hush!" Hannah shouted wearily. "Yes, the girls *are* my responsibility! And they have run away from home! Mistress Woodcutter has had a total collapse. She's been strung tighter than a corset ever since we arrived here, and now I fear losing the girls is more than her poor tired soul can take! I will not add to her burdens by our fighting—understand? Now *please*, go to her! She needs you! I must try to organize a search for the girls."

Finally Samantha understood. "Mister Mark, he gotta be told!" she mumbled, not ever looking directly into

123

Hannah's face.

"The master is out cold—*drunk!*" Hannah responded. "Where is Celia? Can she make coffee?"

Samantha seemed to ignore Hannah as she began to climb the stairs. She yelled, "Celia! Celia! You make coffee —lots of it, and black and strong as it can be!" Hesitating at the top of the stairs, she turned hateful eyes on Hannah. "I's a doin' this—goin' up to Mistress—cause *I* wants to. Not cause of *you* told me to!"

Hannah sighed, "Oh Lord, spare me," as she ran to the shed which held her drunken master.

As she entered the shack, she reeled as if to faint herself. The odor was beyond belief. Propping open the door with a chair and flinging the windows open wide, she immediately went to the pitcher and bowl in the corner. The water in the pitcher was foul and rancid. The slop jar below had not been emptied in who knows how long. She started to the door with the pitcher, but stopped hesitantly.

Why not? she thought, and dumped the entire pitcher on Mark Woodcutter's head. Then she ran out the door to draw fresh water from the well, not waiting to see her master revive.

"What do you think you are doing?" he asked as she re-entered the shed. He sat on the cot holding his head in his hands. His appearance was a shock to Hannah. He had evidently not shaved, or even washed, in several days. The odor about him was wretched. Hannah hesitated only a minute before she threw the second pitcher of water right in his face.

He rose to his feet, sputtering as he staggered toward her. "What in blue blazes? Why, you little—"

Hannah jumped out of the way as he reached for her. He fell headlong, half in and half out of the doorway. Hannah stepped over the clumsy man and ran to the well for more water.

When she returned with this pitcher, Mister Mark sat on the stoop of the shed. Before he could speak to her, she rushed into an apology. As she handed him the girls' note, she continued. "I'm sorry to have treated you cruelly, Master. But drastic circumstances called for drastic measures. You must help me to organize a search for your daughters, for as I've already told you, your wife is totally down with nerves!"

For the first time since their arrival in America, Hannah saw the man Mark Woodcutter had been before he learned of Marta's death. "My God, what have I done?" he mumbled as he read. Hannah thought it was more of a prayer than a curse. He sat, stunned, with tears flowing freely as he read the note. The alcohol muddled his brain, and he begged Hannah. "Help me! What shall we do?"

Hannah thought for a minute. "Could Leroy be trusted to carry a note into Norfolk asking for men to come and search the woods? Surely you have friends who could . . ."

Mister Mark staggered back into the shed. In a few minutes he emerged with a note written on a piece of slate. "Give this to Leroy and tell him to . . . oh! My head!" he groaned, as he fell back against the shed.

"Come on," Hannah pulled on his arm. She steered him toward the kitchen door. "Celia is boiling coffee. While Leroy goes into town, you will drink all of it and clean yourself up." He only had strength enough to nod mutely.

By that afternoon there were several organized search parties combing the land around the house. Two of the groups had barking hound dogs with them. Hannah had found some of the girls' clothing waiting to be washed. These had been held in front of the hounds. Instantly they had taken off toward the west, baying as they went. The men from town carried lanterns, guns, and water canteens. At first Hannah could hear them calling desperately "Karla! Louisa!" but now they were out of earshot.

A doctor had been summoned to her mistress. But, by the time he arrived, he wasn't really needed. Hannah had been sitting at her side and thus was witness to what had affected her quick recovery. The mistress was conscious, to be sure. But a glazed look clouded her eyes. She seemed not to recognize anyone. Not until Mister Mark entered the room.

His hair was still wet, but combed neatly. Hannah noticed that there were a couple of nicks on his face, but it was scrubbed shiny clean. He wore a clean linsey-woolsay shirt tucked into khaki colored breeches. He crossed the width of the room in two strides and fell on his knees beside the bed.

"My darling wife," he choked. "I am so very sorry. Can you ever forgive me?"

Hannah stole from the room as her mistress' voice said, "Oh Mark—you've come home!"

Now Mark led one of the search parties. It had been several hours since the searching had begun in earnest. Darkness was beginning to fall when the mistress entered Hannah's room.

"Hannah," she began to sob. "What if they don't find my angels? I don't think I could—"

Hannah interrupted with a Scripture verse, "Casting all your care upon Him, for He careth for you."

Mistress Woodcutter sighed. "I'd almost forgotten that we could pray." Together they knelt and poured out their longings to God.

Celia kept making pot after pot of coffee. They ate only what they had to, a little bread spread with apple butter every few hours; they drank gallons of coffee. Some of the men came back periodically to see if perhaps they had missed the three shot signal that the girls had been found—

but after a bit of refreshment, they would always go out again.

Dawn was beginning to break in the east. Mistress had finally been persuaded to go back to bed and was dozing a little. Hannah, at her side, snapped to attention when they heard the shot. The men had determined before they left that two shots would signify the girls were found. A third shot would mean, "both are alive and well."

Thus the two women clutched each other's hands. The second shot rang out. Eternity began! What if?

But there was the third shot! The two exhausted ladies fell into each other's arms, crying and laughing hysterically.

Before long, Mark arrived carrying Louisa in his arms. She slept so soundly she never even knew he placed her lovingly in her bed. Behind him came a tall lanky fellow named Chad Witherspoon, carrying a tearfully penitent Karla.

After all the hubbub of supplying food for the search parties and thanking them for their efforts, the house grew quiet at last. It was now full daylight, but the Woodcutter household was retiring for some much needed sleep.

As Hannah was opening her bedroom door, she heard a hoarse whisper from the other end of the hall. Her master and mistress were entering their room together.

"Miss Hannah, thank you for everything!" Mister Mark whispered.

"A belated Merry Christmas to both of you!" Hannah smiled.

From that day forward the atmosphere in the house was idyllic. Hannah's daily goals were nearly always met. The girls were maturing beautifully under her wise leadership. Mealtimes were delightful. The family had begun to frequently entertain guests from Norfolk. A normal routine and happy lifestyle were established. Best of all, now each Sunday the family rode to a lovely little country church and worshiped together. Had it not been for her constant longing for Will, and Samantha's hatred of her, Hannah would have been completely happy.

Three months to the day from the girls' return home, Hannah was braiding Louisa's hair as Karla struggled with her own. The mistress entered the nursery, with a smile from ear to ear.

"What is it, Mama?" Karla asked.

"Girls, I believe that in the fall of this year the Lord is going to give you either another sister or mayhap a brother."

All four ladies squealed and shouted and danced in delight. Down the hallway, Mark Woodcutter smiled.

Chapter 17

ill blinked in the bright sunlight as he stumbled through the door. Mr. Devon sat astride his beautiful horse, dressed all in white, just like yesterday. The horse pawed the ground impatiently, sending little clouds of dust everywhere.

"So, Will Stivers, where are you from?" the master asked.

Will mumbled "Germany." If the man knew how to read, all of the vital statistics about Will were on the Contract of Indentureds he had signed. Surely the man knew all about him.

"Ever work cotton before?" he asked.

"No, sir, but I like to work in the ground and grow things. I think I'll learn about cotton fast." Now that Will was more awake, his amiable spirit was returning.

"Kinda cocky, ain't ya, Stivers?" said the boss.

"I don't mean to be," Will replied. "It's just that I aim to do my best for you, Sir, for I am grateful that you paid my ship fare."

"Don't want your gratitude. Just want your work for the next four years. Now—we work seven days a week here at Devonshire. A wagon comes through the quarters

about one-half hour after sunup. You get on it. My overseer, Cletus, will tell you where you work and what to do
each day. We bring you back to the quarters at about sundown. Then you have about one-half hour before bedding.
Any questions, Stivers?" He obviously didn't expect any,
for he turned the horse to go.

"Yes, sir," Will began hesitantly. "May I please have a
broom?"

Mr. Devon sneered, "No—you may not please have a
broom! This is the quarters, you fool!"

"What difference does that—Sir, I do not understand
why you would want us to be dirty."

"Shows what you know, Stivers! It ain't that I want you
to be dirty. It's just that a broom could be used as a club
or any other kind of weapon by these uncivilized Nigras.
They might revolt. We can't allow anything down here
that the slaves could use against us!"

Evidently the man was paranoid where his slaves were
concerned.

"But, I'm not a slave," Will insisted. "And I wouldn't
hurt you nor—"

"Forget it, Stivers!" shouted his boss impatiently. "For the
next four years you may as well consider yourself a slave.
You'll be treated just like the rest of these sorry creatures
down here. Do you have any other questions?" he barked.

"Well—not a question exactly. Just a statement. You
said we're to work seven days a week. Well, I can't. I
mean—I won't! For, you see, I'm a Christian and I believe
it is a sin to work on the day God has set aside for us to
rest and worship Him. I will not work on Sunday!"

Mr. Devon stared incredulously. "You must be joking!"
he exclaimed.

"No, sir, I'm serious. This is my conviction and you
cannot make me go against my beliefs!" Will replied con-
fidently.

"Stivers, this has gone far enough. You will do whatever you're ordered to do or else you will be sorry. This is Thursday. In three days from now, you'd better be on that wagon heading to the field with the rest of the crew . . . or else you'll wish you had! Understand?"

Will just stared at the man for his answer. Suddenly a big bell rang on the corner of a crude shelter Will had not noticed the night before. Mr. Devon spurred the horse and raced out across the field. The bell rang again and Will saw Liza in the shelter.

"Bell means breakfast, German! Come and get it."

Will hustled into the shelter and received a big steaming bowl of the whitest oatmeal he'd ever seen. Now others—many, many blacks and some mulattos, shuffled toward the hut. There were many strong-looking young men. The women, who were evidently their wives, were herding children of all sizes toward the food. Many of the ladies had a baby suckling at their bare breast. Will found himself embarrassed, and turned away red-faced. Silently, he wondered why he felt this way. He knew nursing a child was the most natural act on earth.

Will tasted the oatmeal and he must have unconsciously made a face.

"What's wrong, Germ? You don't care for grits? Better learn to like them. It's every-morning fare here at Demonland," Liza taunted him good-naturedly.

After swallowing what he could of the awful tasting grits, Will returned the bowl to the end of Liza's serving table as he'd seen others of the silent blacks doing.

"Why does no one talk?" he asked Liza.

"Most of dem don't speak de same language. Hardly none of dem speaks English. The rest—well, what is there to say?" came the response.

Will shrugged. Suddenly he remembered the squalor in his cabin.

"Miss Liza, where did you say I could get water?"

She pointed to the well at the other end of the compound. "Better hurry, Germ. Wagon coming soon."

Will just had enough time to haul two buckets of water to his new home and throw the water in an arc on the floor before he heard the wagon. He turned dejectedly away from the mud he'd just made, and then climbed aboard with all the others.

They rode nearly half an hour before the wagon pulled up in a stump-ridden, swampy field. There were twenty men left off to work in this field and the wagon went on, out of sight. While riding, Will had met a friendly brown fellow named "Solly"—short for Solomon, he presumed. Cletus, the overseer, carried a menacing whip and had a pistol stuck in his belt. Obviously he was not to be trifled with. Will was surprised when Cletus had ordered half of them out of the wagon. Where was the cotton? Soon he discovered that his task today was to be working on stump removals in this field "so that Mr. Devon can plant more of the white."

Solly became Will's partner. They lit fires around the bottoms of some of the stumps, to which they constantly added leaves and twigs. Using the crude shovels that Cletus had given out as they jumped off the wagon, they dug as deeply as they could around the stumps that had already been burned.

Solly and Will became fast friends as they labored. After telling of his own life, Will learned that Solly was a slave. He told his story in broken English and said that he had been hunting in his homeland across great waters when a net fell on him. Then he was on a ship. Large tears slid down his cheeks when he told Will he had a wife and three boys in Africa.

The sun was high overhead when Solly stopped digging around the stumps' roots. "Is enough," he motioned to

Will.

"Nigras!" he shouted at an ear-splitting level. "Y'all come—we pull!"

Now Will understood. There had been one rope dropped in the field by Cletus. Solly tied it securely several times through the roots of the old stump they'd uncovered that morning. Now the men made a single-file line and put the rope over all their shoulders. "Pull," Solly yelled. All twenty of them strained forward. Sweat stood out on foreheads. Groaning ran along the line. "Pull," he yelled again. After several seconds of straining they would all relax. Evidently these men had worked together thus oftentimes before. *Doing the work of oxen or draft horses*, Will thought in disgust.

Will felt a rhythm developing in the earth beneath him. The men were all stomping their feet as they strained to pull the stubborn stump. And now it became musical. First only Solly sang. Then slowly the others joined in.

Will didn't understand. They half hummed "Oh me oh my oh me oh"—the same syllables over and over. The vowel sounds changed but the tune, sung in a minor key, remained the same. He soon joined in the workers' crude dance and song.

Solly screamed, "She comes!" and a shout rose from the crowd on the rope. Suddenly Will realized that the line of men was moving rather than stomping in place. They drug the heavy stump to an ash heap where others had been burned in the past. About then a small wagon lumbered into the field.

"Nooning!" shouted the little boy who drove. Again the men lined up solemnly. At the wagon each was handed an apple and a tin cup of water. Evidently this was their lunch.

And so the day continued. Will spent much of his time slapping at the pesky mosquitoes which seemed to plague him much more than his dark-skinned companions.

By the time the wagon pulled up to take them home, Will was famished. Every muscle in his tired body ached. He pulled himself into the wagon with a groan.

Back in the quarters, they were served a bowl of delicious stew and a chunk of corn bread. It didn't come close to assuaging his hunger, but at least it helped.

Will staggered toward his filthy home, dreading to see the muddy mess he'd left that morning. There was just enough light for him to be greatly surprised when he walked through the doorway. There was a strong smell of lye soap, and the floor was spotless. His clothing was all hanging neatly on nails he hadn't seen before. And, perhaps best of all, there was a soft cotton comforter atop his cornhusk mattress. He blinked in shock and fell on the crude stool in the corner.

"Who—and why?" he mumbled, wondering for a brief second if he was in the wrong cabin.

"I done it," said Liza from outside. "I snuck down here while Cletus and Devon was gone today."

"But why?" Will asked, staggering tiredly to the door.

"Don't rightly know. Never did see a man hanker so much to be clean. And, Germ, you 'minds me of my son, Booker. Even though you's white, you looks a lot like my baby what Mr. Devon done sold off from me five year ago. So I like you." With tear-filled eyes, she was off at a run for the big house.

As Will fell atop the cot that night, he tried to thank God for the day. But in truth all he could be thankful for was Liza's unrequested act of kindness in his behalf. In the middle of his prayer, panic seized him. He jumped up and stumbled around in the dark searching for his valise. When he finally found it, it was empty. They weren't there! He felt his way over to the hooks on the wall and went through all the pockets. Just as he was about to despair, he felt on the sort of shelf made where the roof overhung the top of the wall. There, just above the clothing on the hooks, lay his lovely soft white wool mittens. Foolishly, for the night was warm, he put them on. Returning to his cot, he fell almost instantly into a deep sleep. It was to become a nightly ritual. For four long years, he vowed to sleep in mittens!

* * * * * * * * * * *

"It's been a year, Stivers! When are you going to give in?" Cletus mumbled as once again he strapped Will to the whipping post which stood in the middle of the row of houses in the quarters.

"Never!" Will replied.

"I hate this. If Mr. Devon didn't make me . . ."

"I know. It's your job. Don't worry."

"But why, man? What has God ever done for you to deserve such loyalty? All Devon wants is for you to go to the fields on Sunday with the others. I won't make you work when you get there."

"It's the principle of it, Cletus. Just get it over with, will you?"

So once again Cletus raised the great bull whip ten times to Will's bare back. In the early days Will had fainted every week when he was whipped. It still hurt beyond belief, but somehow Will felt peace in spite of the pain as he bathed his bleeding back each week. Lately he noticed it didn't even bleed as much. The scar tissue was nearly an inch thick. He guessed that was why he walked with stooped shoulders now.

Other than the beatings, the year had not been too bad. He knew he had lost a lot of weight, for his clothes hung on him. He'd learned all about cotton—when to plant, when to harvest, and how to weed and cultivate it. And during the off-season there were always fields to clear of stumps.

He'd developed a close friendship with Solly and the black women the master had ordered Solly to bed with. Master Devon used Solly as a virtual stud service, treating him like a prime race horse. Again Will thanked God he'd been spared that duty. He never could have returned to Hannah had Devon forced him into adultery. Thankfully, he only wanted to breed full Negroes, believing them to be better workers than mulattos.

It was well into his second year at Demonland when one day Will passed out in the field. They laid him under a tree till the nooning wagon came. By the time the boy driver turned him over to Liza, he was delirious with fever—a bad case of malaria. When he was recovering, Cletus ordered him to help Liza in the cook house till he was strong enough to work the fields.

As he peeled potatoes for her, she giggled, "Who is your Miss Hannah, Germ? And what's she got to do with them mittens?"

Will was startled. How did Liza know of the mittens—or Hannah?

"I snuck down to nurse you when the fever was worst, Germ. And when Cletus and me was ordered to burn all your clothes to rid the quarters of malaria, you clung to them mittens a sayin' 'Oh no, Miss Hannah. I'll never lose them. Never!' Cletus, he said he thinks it's the bugs what causes the disease anyway 'stead of clothes and such—so we let you keep yo mittens."

Will didn't want to tell Liza his life story. So he replied thoughtfully, "Once I knew a girl—a wonderful girl—named Hannah. And the mittens—they are a kind of symbol to me. A symbol of love . . . and of freedom in the future."

The next day Cletus ordered Will back to the fields. As he climbed off the wagon with others, Cletus detained him. "Your illness was a blessing, Stivers."

136

"What do you mean?"

"Well, Devon heard how sick you were and said if you didn't die, I could stop the beatings. Said he guessed a live worker six days a week was better'n a dead one. Doubt you could stand a beating now, as sick as you've been. Guess you won, Will!" He saluted playfully.

Will smiled thoughtfully. "Just a battle, Cletus—not the war!" he said as he headed into a great field of white.

Chapter 18

annah could hardly believe that over half of her time to be spent with the Woodcutter family was gone. So many changes had taken place, and yet life continued. Sometimes she felt that her youth was passing by as a cat slinks round a barn at night. Never had this feeling been more poignant than last August on the bittersweet day when Karla had been married.

Of course the day had been anticipated for more than the entire year previous to it. For it seemed that from that awful day after Christmas of 1752 when Chad Witherspoon had carried Karla home, until the wedding, he had always been about. He had truly been smitten with what the poets called "love at first sight." Karla, on the other hand, had taken some convincing.

Now, as Hannah recalled their courtship, she smiled wistfully. "'Twasn't so much that Karla had to be made to love Chad as 'twas that she had some growing up to do," she mumbled.

That first winter in America, Chad had dropped by as often as the weather permitted. He always wore snowshoes, whether there was snow or not. Hannah expected it had been to try to impress Karla though Chad claimed 'twas easier to walk the woodland trail to Norfolk in the clumsy webbed affairs than in just regular boots. Karla, Louisa, and Chad were forever heard shouting and romping through games of tag and blind man's bluff in the yard.

"'Tain't right. Dem girls s'posed to be young ladies by now, a trainin' themselves to be young wifes and mothers. And they's out a-rompin' in the yard wif dat boy!" Samantha often grumbled. Perhaps it was due to the feeling that she'd lost her own youth, or maybe it was just to overrule Samantha—whatever the reason, Hannah, as governess, allowed and even encouraged the playtime with Chad.

But come June, all the playing had stopped. Chad announced one evening at dinner that the next day was his eighteenth birthday.

"Eighteen, eh?" Mister Mark had been surprised. "What do you plan to do with your life, Chad?"

"Beginning tomorrow I shall work full time aside my father in the glass works of Norfolk. 'Tis a hot dirty job, to be sure, but one that pays fairly well. Enough for a man to support a family on," he added with a meaningful wink in Karla's direction. Karla had only looked confused.

Later that night Hannah had overheard this conversation from the girls' room.

"He's dreamy! Oh Karla, you two will have such beautiful babies!"

"Sister, how you talk! Why, he's just Chad—our playmate, our pal! I could never consider marrying him!"

Karla's tune had begun to change the very next week. She'd been depressed and despondent all day. Hannah had grown concerned and asked, "Are you sick, Karla?"

Louisa teased, "She's lovesick, that's what!"

Karla burst into tears. "'Tis *not* lovesickness! Can't a girl miss having a friend come to play without being accused of being in love?"

But when Chad finally appeared ten days later, on his first day off, Hannah noticed that instead of playing games, he and Karla took a long walk in the woods. Hannah's eyes grew misty remembering her own walks through the woods of Germany with Will.

Thus, what began as a childhood friendship had grown into a beautiful love. Both young people had been sensible, however. Though the engagement became official on Christmas of 1753, being announced at a glorious ball given by Karla's parents, the wedding hadn't taken place until this last August. While Karla spent the intervening time filling a hope chest with finely embroidered linen, Chad had overseen construction of a lovely cottage halfway into Norfolk from the Woodcutters.

Hannah knew she would never forget Karla's wedding day. It seemed God himself must have planned the weather, for the sky had never been bluer, the air never clearer. The temperature was just right also. And even the humidity was almost non-existent, very rare in August.

First down the long stairway came Louisa, looking ready to be a bride herself. She wore a blue dress exactly the color of her eyes, and her long blonde hair was braided, with strands of honeysuckle and baby's breath woven in. She carried yellow baby roses. Hannah thought her title for that day fit perfectly, for she truly looked like a maid of honor. After Louisa took her place near Chad and the minister in the foyer, all eyes gazed aloft again.

Now Mister Mark and his beautiful almost fifteen-year-old daughter appeared. There was an audible sigh as the small crowd beheld the beaming duo descending the stairs regally. Karla's dress was of the most flawless white satin. Every seed pearl which outlined the bodice had been double-stitched by Mistress Woodcutter herself. A veil of bridal illusion was held in place by rosettes of the same satin as the dress. But, all the details of the dress had been forgotten when one looked at her face. Never had it been more obvious that little Karla had grown up. The love which jumped from her eyes to rest on Chad was the deep lasting kind, Hannah was sure.

The ceremony was beautiful until little ten-month-old Marcus decided it had gone on long enough. Just as the minister was declaring Chad and Karla to be "husband and wife together," the stillness was shattered by an ear-splitting bellow. For a few seconds, everyone grew flustered. Instinctively, Hannah had taken control of the situation. She grabbed baby Marcus from the arms of her mistress, whispered "We'll go outside," and slipped out almost unnoticed by the guests.

"I almost feel I should thank you, little Marc," she choked between sobs. Thankfully, no one else had seen how the ceremony had upset Hannah. "Oh Marcus, two years is such a long time! Does he still remember me and love me? Is he sick or hurt, or . . . is he even still alive? How can I stand it?" she sobbed against a post in the barn. It was the only time since leaving Norfolk that Hannah had completely lost control of her emotions about Will. And little Marc, the only witness to this outburst, sat in the hay, surrounded by barn kittens, totally oblivious to Hannah.

She regained control of herself and carried little Marc out back to the well where she washed her face as well as his. Then together they sneaked back in to enjoy the reception with the other family and friends.

"Samantha, the food is delicious," Hannah tried once more to befriend the slave. "'Tis the prettiest cake I've ever seen."

The great black woman nearly spat in her face. "I does *my* part! Too bad the governess couldn't keep the baby from spoilin' Miss Karla's beautiful ceremony!"

Now, four months later, the house was all astir with excitement over Christmas, only five days away. Karla and Chad would come and spend the entire week from Christmas till New Year's with the Woodcutters. But perhaps even more exciting was that Mister Mark's brother, Captain Phillip of the *Wedgewood*, was also to arrive shortly. He had never visited the mansion since their arrival, though Hannah heard periodically through the visitors from Norfolk that the *Wedgewood* was in the harbor.

Hannah felt responsible for Captain Phillip's approaching visit. One evening she came across a brooding Mister Mark on the porch. It was dusk and Hannah wouldn't have seen him, had he not spoken.

"Miss Hannah, have you a moment?"

"Yes, sir. What is it you wish?"

She was surprised at his emotion as he replied. "Peace, Hannah—I want peace of mind and heart." She knew not how to answer him.

"I . . . I . . . thought you'd made your peace with God, Master," she stammered.

"I have made it, *with God!* I know now that 'tis no one's fault we lost Marta. And God has been good to us. He gave us little Marc. And Chad and Karla are so happy. I only wish . . . I only wish I could go back and take back some things I said to my brother two years ago."

"Oh, I see," Hannah had said. "Well, can't you?"

"We Woodcutters have always been proud stubborn men. If I were to apologize to Phil . . . well, he'd think 'I'd gone daft. But . . . I cannot sleep or eat or think. I keep hearing myself saying 'I never want to see you again. You murdered my baby.' Now, I wish . . . oh, I'd give just about anything to see him."

So Hannah set her plan in motion and sent word, via

Leroy, that Captain Phillip was invited to spend Christmas at the mansion. She'd conspired with the mistress, and between them they had decided it was time for a reunion between the brothers. So, as a Christmas surprise to Mark, they had planned it all.

Fleetingly, Hannah wondered if the ship captain would agree to come, but thankfully he had. Now, as the day approached, Hannah was as excited as the children.

Christmas Day dawned bright, clear and crisp. Louisa was sharing the nursery with Hannah, because Chad and Karla were still sleeping in the girls' room. Hannah tiptoed down the hallway, holding tightly to Louisa's hand. They didn't wish to waken anyone, especially little Marc, whose anticipation of today had kept him awake hours past his bedtime last evening.

"Hannah, what do you think Papa will do when he sees Uncle Phillip?" Louisa whispered as they went downstairs. She was feeling especially grown-up because her mama had let her in on the secret.

Before Hannah could open her mouth to answer, they heard a shout of "It's Kissmas!" from above. Though the toddling little Marcus could not say the word, he knew that it meant a day of fun and excitement.

Two hours later the family sat in the drawing room, already tiring but happy and relaxed. There had been a bountiful breakfast. Ham, pancakes, scrambled eggs, fried potatoes, scones, and some of Samantha's famous breakfast beef, pounded thin, floured, and fried. There was also gravy and delicious fresh-baked biscuits. If anyone left the table hungry, 'twas their own fault.

Then the doors had been opened upon the drawing room. As if by magic, a huge fir tree had been placed in the center of the south wall and decorated overnight. Under it stood mounds of wrapped presents, most of which were for little Marcus, the darling of the family.

Leroy had spent hours carving and sanding a gorgeous wooden carriage and horse. The little boy was entranced and clapped his hands in glee when shown that by pulling on a string, he could make the toy follow him at will. Karla and Chad had brought him a set of blocks which nested inside each other.

The adults all exchanged small items. Hannah had knit fascinators and stocking caps for the ladies and gentlemen respectively. Everyone remarked about her fine workmanship, which pleased her. She never ceased to be amazed that they all *did* treat her as a member of the family. It was especially evident today as Hannah exchanged gifts with the family. Leroy, Celia, and Samantha were each just handed an orange and a new garment before being dismissed. Hannah was admiring the book of poetry her mistress had given her when suddenly the silence in the room startled her. She looked up to see Captain Phillip in the doorway, resplendent in his dress blue captain's uniform. Everyone was silent. The captain's face grew red, and he stared at the floor.

"Merry Christmas, family," he mumbled.

In two strides, Mister Mark was across the floor. He grabbed his brother in a bear hug. "Phillip!" he exclaimed. "I'm *so* glad you're here!"

Hannah noticed there were tears on his cheeks. Immediately the room became an uproar of greetings. Perhaps only Hannah heard when her master whispered, "I'm sorry, Phil." The smile on the other's face told of the ready forgiveness in his heart.

The captain had gifts for all of them, except little Marc whom he hadn't known existed. But the baby took possession of the captain's hat and was content. Phillip also looked content when Mark placed the wee boy on his lap saying, "Meet your nephew, brother. This is Marcus Phillip Woodcutter."

Captain Phillip had shyly given her a beautiful lace mantilla from Spain. Hannah knew her embarrassment was evident. "But, I have nothing for you, Captain Phillip. I never dreamed—"

"Your invitation to come was a wondrous gift, lassie. 'Tis happy I am just to be able to see ye again!"

Hannah's frustration grew, for it seemed the captain watched her every move and was forever at her side the next few days. She kept hoping she was misreading his motives until late the second night when Louisa said, "Hannah, I think my uncle loves you."

"Oh no! It cannot be. You are wrong, Louisa!" Hannah responded. "Go to sleep, child!"

Louisa giggled. Hannah did not sleep well all that night. She arose early, and hoped a walk in the cold air would clear her senses.

"I've just been imagining it," she said aloud when she stopped for breath in a clearing.

"Imagining what?" said Phillip, some ten feet behind her.

Hannah jumped impulsively and cried out in fear. Immediately he was at her side.

"I'm sorry, Miss Hannah. I never meant to scare ye. But I needed to talk at ye alone, so I followed. Will ye forgive me?"

She relaxed. "Of course," she replied as she sat on a rock.

He knelt beside the rock. Hannah knew her fears were well-founded.

He said, "Miss Hannah, I know this is not the time or place but I must tell ye afore I burst. I love ye. I have since that first storm at sea when I saw the kind of courage ye have inside of ye. No—please—don't interrupt! Let me say m' piece. I know the life of a sailor's wife is lonely and unhappy, but I think brother Mark will let us live on here with him. When I *am* at home, Miss Hannah, I would make ye happy. I know I could! Please, would ye consider bein' my wife?"

It was a beautiful speech. He'd stared at the ground ever since he began, so he could not see how agitated Hannah had become. Now she rose and took three steps before turning anguished eyes on him.

"Captain Phillip—how could you? You, of all people, know that I can never . . ." Her voice broke and she choked back a sob of frustration.

"Oh lassie! Ye certainly aren't still thinking about that German boy, Stivers, are ye? Why, I figured when ye had to be separated all that would be forgotten," he explained tenderly.

"Forgotten!" Her blue eyes snapped, making her even lovelier in the cold morning air. "I shall never forget him! He is my . . . my . . . well, he will be my husband. In only twenty-two more months!"

"But, ye cannot know that for sure, lassie!" he replied. "Ye'll probably never see him again. Why, how on God's earth do ye expect to ever find him again? He's working hundreds of miles south of here."

"We made plans," she answered determinedly. "We're going to meet at—oh! I don't have to tell you! I know he'll be there! He loves me, and I love him! We promised!"

Now the captain grew fatherly in his manner. "I don't doubt that, Miss Hannah. But it has been two long years. Mayhap his feeling has changed for ye."

"Never!" she snapped.

"But Hannah," he exclaimed, dropping the formality in frustration. "I can give ye happiness now! Stivers cannot guarantee anything to ye. I love ye, Hannah. Please consider my proposal!"

"There's nothing to consider, Captain. My heart belongs to another!"

"Another who may be dead!" he shouted in desperation. "I didn't want to tell ye this, but ye force it. The man who purchased your Will's services two year ago works for the meanest man on God's earth. I didn'a know it at the time or I wouldn'a have sold to him. He was the buyer for a man known as 'Demon' all along the coast. Your Will may not even be alive by now."

Hannah's heart wrenched within her. For a second, she wondered if he was lying to further his cause, but she knew instinctively he was sincere, and began to cry.

"Sweetheart, don't!" he begged, awkwardly patting her back. "I'm sorry to tell ye, but Hannah ye shouldn't wait for anyone sold to the Demon. Marry me, and we will be happy *now!*"

She turned sad blue eyes at him. "I cannot, Captain Phillip. I'm honored that you've asked me. Truly I am. But I love Will. I must wait for him. Try to understand."

They stood for the slightest moment, staring at each other.

With a quick nod, he turned and ran back to the house. Hannah spent the morning in the woods, knowing the family was still in a holiday spirit and deserved time alone. When she returned at lunch time, the mistress greeted her.

"Hannah, you've just missed seeing Phillip off. He decided he'd best get back to the ship and set sail while the winds were favorable. He asked me to bid you adieu for him."

Hannah did not expect the great sense of loss that enveloped her. *Could he be right?* she wondered. *Is Will . . . did I make a mistake?*

Chapter 19

ill was recovering from another of his endless bouts with malaria. His fever had been high again during the night. He'd dreamed fitfully, first of Hannah, then of Cletus with the whip, then of Liza taking his mittens away. He awoke shaking with chills and drenched with sweat. He knew by now that when the heavy sweating began, he would feel better soon. He couldn't even remember how many times he'd been stricken with the disease.

Cletus, who by now had become a good friend to Will, stopped the wagon directly in front of Will's hut.

"Stivers, how goes it?" he shouted.

Will staggered to the doorway and braced himself against it as he answered. "I'm better today. Mayhap I could try to come to the fields."

"Are you crazy, man?" the overseer retorted. "Stay here and try to get your strength back. Demon is gone down to the city and won't be back till at least tomorrow. So he'll never need to know you've been sick again iff'n ye get well by tomorrow." He turned his attention to the wagonload of slaves. "Everybody here? Okay, let's go!" With a crack of the whip to the horses, they were gone.

Will stared after the wagon. He had almost learned not to mind the horrid living conditions here at Demonland. In fact, it had begun to seem like home. "Until Solly . . ." he mumbled, the memories returning in a flood of emotion. "Oh Solly," Will cried. "Why did it have to happen?"

Solly had become Will's dearest friend on earth. They'd worked together every day. Solly was the only person with whom Will had shared all his hopes and dreams of a future with Hannah. They ate every meal sitting side by side. On good days they teased Liza playfully. Solly often had bad days when he seemed all inside of himself, and Will knew his heart and mind were across the waters with his wife and sons. Will tried to cheer him on those days, but Solly would snap at him.

"Oh Weel," he would stammer in his broken English, "you don know how it makes me feel to be used like a horse or a bull. I's the father of p'obly twenty chilluns on this land, but I's not 'llowed to act like a father to none of dem. Ain't right!"

Of course Will had no answer for Solly's plight, so at these times he would just pat the great black's back and say, "God cares, Solly. And I care. I only wish . . ."

Will had no idea when Solly had decided to run away from Demonland. True, there had been a noticeable change in the man. When he spoke of his homeland his eyes sparkled like stars. Will would never forget the one day Solly had been so animated.

"Weel," he'd whispered as they'd knelt weeding the cotton. "Dem boats what bringed us peoples here from Affica—dey goes back to steal more of us, doesn't they?"

"Well yes, I suppose," Will replied. "But why . . .?"

"Den I's goin' back, Weel. I don know how or when but I's goin'!"

A few nights later Will had almost been asleep when he felt an awkward nudge on his foot.

"Weel, Weel . . . I's goin'. I's sorry to leave you, my friend. But just like you has to continue in this awful place for your Hannah's sake, I's got to leave it for the sake of my Treeka and my boys."

Now Will was fully awake. "But how will you . . . where . . .?"

"I's goin' toward the risin' sun all de time. When I gets to the big water, I'll just hunt till I finds a boat goin' back to my home. Den I'll find me a place to hide on dat boat."

Will tried to interrrupt to point out to Solly all the holes in his plan, but the big man said, "No more time now, Weel. I has to go tween Cletus' rounds of patrollin'. I . . . uh, goodbye Weel!"

The two friends embraced. Will was embarrassed to find tears on his face after Solly ran from his cabin door.

Will's mind lurched ahead from that time to the present and he pondered anew the question that had plagued him.

Who could have reported him? Even now, several months after the incident, Will was consumed with ill feelings toward whoever it was.

It was a few hours after Solly had escaped that Will heard the sickening baying of the hounds on his trail.

"Oh God, let him make it!" Will prayed. But 'twas to no avail. Not fifteen minutes later two shots rang out, and the nightmare was only beginning.

Near morning, the mealtime bell rang frantically. The street between the quarters was well lit by torches. Mr. Devon had charged around on his beautiful horse shouting, "Nigras! Get out of your beds and get out here! Now! I wants you to see what happens to people who try to run away from Devonshire!"

As the people emerged from the cabins, women screamed, children fainted, and even the strongest men retched. For there in the middle of the street on the post where Will had taken so many beatings, was the head of their friend Solly. A cold realization of their own condition took shape in their minds as they watched. The man who owned the plantation was a demon who had beheaded a man because he wanted to be free.

Now several months later, as Will watched the wagon going to the field, it all came back to him. He stumbled over to his bed blinking back tears. He wrapped the thin blanket around him as the chills began. Thankfully, he fell asleep again.

When next he awoke, Liza was there with a bowl of steaming broth.

"Best eat this, Germ. Ye needs some nourishment."

He sat up and sipped the hot liquid. "It's good, Liza. Thank you."

She sat down on the stool and fanned herself. "Sure be hot for this time of year."

"What time of year is it, Liza? I've been so sick that I've lost all track of time. How long have I been sick?"

She chuckled. "Christmas Day is only one week away. I knows cause Mr. Devon, he been fattening a big ole Tom Turkey and I's supposed to ring he neck and stuff he and bake he for the big house one week from today."

Will was confused. "Do you know what year it is?"

Now Liza didn't understand.

"I came here in 1752. Have I been here two Christmases or three? With all the beatings that first year and all the times I've had this wretched illness, I don't know about the time. Liza, I *have* to know! What year is this?" he shouted frantically.

"Easy, Germ, easy! I don't know—I never knew they numbered years. Is that what white people means when they talk bout birfdays?"

"Oh Liza," Will sighed in exasperation. "How can I find out? Mayhap my time is done. Mayhap . . ."

From the doorway came an angry shout. Neither Liza

nor Will had heard the eavesdropper.

"Your time ain't done for ten more months, Stivers! So don't get in no hurry to leave me, else you'll end up like Solly. Woman, what are you doing in there?" Mr. Devon pinched Liza's arm as she side-stepped to the door.

"Just brung the Germ some broth, Master Devon. He been taken with the malaria again."

"Don't look too sick to me, Stivers. When the boy takes the noonin' wagon to the fields, you be on it! Give me at least half a day's work. Fakin' malaria is pretty low, Stivers," he said as he backed out of the hut.

To himself he mumbled, "Gonna have me a talk with that Cletus. No wonder my crop is way down if this is how he oversees my place. Lettin' one of my best workers lay around pretendin' to be sick!"

Will tried to feel joy at the knowledge that Devon thought of him as "one of my best workers." He reminded himself that the Bible said whatever he did, he should do it as unto the Lord. But even then he was filled with disgust. "I'll do it for You, Lord, but I wish that Devon the demon did not benefit by what I do for You," he prayed.

Wearily he dressed himself, then waited in the sunlight for the nooning wagon to come.

* * * * * * * * * * *

A quiet year had passed at the Woodcutters. Karla and Chad were frequent dinner guests, or had been until the last several weeks. For now Karla was eagerly anticipating the birth of her first child. She had grown extremely uncomfortable as her tiny waist disappeared and her figure ballooned. So for the past few weeks she had stayed at home.

Even Christmas had been quiet. Hannah had of course been invited to go with the family to Karla's home. But when she determined through conversations around her that Captain Phillip had also been invited, she dogmatically refused to go.

"You need time to be alone with just the family," she'd insisted to her bewildered mistress.

"But we think of you as our family."

"I know, and I appreciate that. But in actuality we all know that in ten short months I will be leaving you. So I'd best stay at home this holiday."

Hannah knew the family was hurt. And yet, she could not face seeing Captain Phillip Woodcutter again.

Though quiet, it had been a troubled year for Hannah. She'd lost weight and often was so listless she even forgot to set daily goals in the morning. She dreamed and daydreamed of Will being tortured to death. She found herself crying for no good reason. Her faith in the ability of God to work things out for her good began to waver.

The entire family was thankful for little Marcus these days. For without Karla's carefree attitude to bolster their spirits, 'twas often only Marcus that brightened their days. Louisa had become a silent, morose creature whom Hannah could no longer understand.

One night Hannah heard sobbing from across the hall. "Miss Louisa, what is it?" Hannah asked as she wrapped the girl in her arms.

"Oh Hannah, I'm so lonely. I miss Karla so much. I love little Marc, but he makes me so nervous with all his loud playing. I feel so . . . so . . . oh Hannah, David is going to marry Cynthia! And I love him so much!"

Hannah sat speechless with dismay. Evidently Louisa had secretly loved David Ingalls, the carpenter who'd recently worked three weeks repairing storm damage on the barn. He was ten years older than Louisa, so no one had payed any attention to her insistence on helping him. Now she cried of a broken heart over his approaching nuptial.

The next morning, Hannah suggested to her mistress that Louisa be sent to stay with Karla till the baby arrived. The Woodcutters, upon hearing Hannah's reasons, agreed that a change of scenery would be good for their daughter. Thus, Louisa had stayed at the Witherspoons on Christmas. This left Hannah with much free time on her hands, her only responsibility now being little Marcus who napped both morning and afternoon.

On New Year's Day the little boy ran down the hall-way shouting, "Hannah! Hannah! He's here. The man with the wondrous hat is here. Come, Hannah—he wants to see you!"

Hannah's heart nearly stopped. Marcus was wearing a sea captain's hat. "Come on, Hannah!" he insisted.

She patted her hair in place and let the child pull her down the stairs.

"Hello Miss Hannah," he said.

If only he weren't so handsome, she thought. She tried to bring to her memory a picture of Will, but it had been over three years since she had last seen him. And here, directly in front of her, stood the other man who loved her!

"Captain, shall we sit down?" she managed to say though her thoughts were reeling.

"Hannah, you said I could play outside!" Marcus insisted, dragging his boots and leggings. She bundled the boy and as he romped in the two-inch snowfall, she sat with the captain on the porch.

"Ye look lovely," he said.

"Thank you—but, please . . ." She turned sad eyes on him.

"Alright—I can already see that ye have not changed your mind. Well, let me tell ye what I've come to, and then quickly be gone." He strode to the edge of the porch

154

and did not look at her as he talked. "I did not sail back to the Motherland as I'd planned when I left here last year. Instead, I left the *Wedgewood* at anchor in the harbor for nigh onto four months. During that time I searched hither and yon trying to get information about this man known as Demon, who is your Will's master. I finally found the plantation known as Devonshire. I was able to talk with the man who used to be the buyer of slaves and indentureds—name of Hank Scott. He lives on a small farm of his own now, near the big plantation. Seems he plays poker once a week with Devon's overseer, a man named Cletus. According to this man, Cletus—but this was last spring mind ye—your Will Stivers is still alive and well. This Cletus told Hank that Will has been through a lot—uh, sickness mostly . . ." (he maintained his resolve not to tell her about the beatings) "but said he's never seen a man with more spunk and will to live. Cletus told Hank he had heard that Stivers was determined to stay alive for a gal of his up north. Guess that must be ye, Hannah." The captain turned to face her with so much love in his eyes that she looked away, embarrassed.

"Oh Phillip," she wept unashamedly. "How can I ever thank you? You've given me renewed hope to go on. I can face anything if I know that my darling Will . . ." But here she hesitated for her very words seemed to cut the man before her to the heart.

He shook his head sadly. "Don't thank me. I don't know why I did it. I did not find the answers I had hoped for. I know I can never be happy, but I do long for ye to be happy, Hannah. Because, I love ye."

With that he bounded off the porch. "Give me back m' cap, little Marcus Phillip. I have to go now."

Hannah brushed the snow off the little boy as the captain mounted up. "Thank you," she called as he rode out of the clearing. If he heard, he made no response.

155

The next ten months flew by. Louisa came home in April having grown from a heartbroken girl to a lovely young woman. She'd cared tenderly for her sister and baby Marta, and at the same time she herself had fallen in love with Chad Witherspoon's younger brother, Daniel. Their whirlwind courtship had climaxed with a beautiful wedding, again in August.

Hannah's goal for every day of her last two months with the Woodcutters was the same. "Today I shall make a friend of Samantha!"

But, day by day, the big black lady rebuffed her acts of kindness. When Hannah would compliment the food, Samantha snapped, "I does my job!" When Hannah offered to help in the kitchen one day, the slave shouted, "Get outta my kitchen, you white trash! You thinks you's something! A member of de family! Well, you ain't nothin' but a charity case!"

Hannah stood her ground. "Why do you hate me so Samantha?"

"You knows why! Now, get outta my . . ."

"No, Samantha. I don't know why. What have I ever done to you?"

"Ain't what you done. It's what you is! In a couple mo' months, you gonna be free to walk down de big road. Me, I ain't never . . . Now get outta my way!" She had pushed, choking back a sob.

"But Mister Mark is a good master. He never . . ."

"Sho he good. But he a master all de same. Now I's tellin' you for de last time, you white trash, git outta my kitchen!"

Because she'd picked up a butcher knife, Hannah retreated. Finally understanding the slave's problem, she gave her a wide berth. She knew her goal of befriending the Negro was one she would never meet. *Guess all I can do is pray for her*, she thought.

* * * * * * * * * * *

It was October 26, 1756. In two faraway places, two people bade their farewells. Will from abject squalor and Hannah from a loving family.

Will never saw Mr. Devon at all. Cletus rode him on the back of his horse to the main gate of the plantation. Will carried only a small gunnysack with some foodstuffs Liza had secretly prepared. The sack also held, wrapped securely in brown paper, the white mittens which Liza had laundered as a last act of kindness to her "Germ." Will jumped down at the gate. Cletus handed him the manumission papers and shook his hand.

"Good luck, Will Stivers. It's been a pleasure to know you."

"Goodbye, Cletus," Will responded. He stood for a minute watching as Cletus trotted back toward the quarters.

"This time, old Cletus—this time I won the war!" With the biggest smile on his face in four years, he began his long trek northward.

At the Woodcutters, the mistress was teary-eyed. "You *will* come back to visit us, won't you Hannah? I still can't believe you are leaving. If you would only stay . . ."

Hannah interrupted. "Oh Mistress, of course I'll be back. I'll only be living in Norfolk. I'll send word via the Witherspoon boys as to where I'll be staying. I . . . uh—I guess the time has come . . ." Though excited to see Will, Hannah was also going to miss this adopted family of hers dearly.

Mister Mark sat in the driver's seat of a small buggy which carried Hannah's trunks. He cleared his throat meaningfully.

"Goodbye Mistress," Hannah said, hurriedly hugging her. "Little Marcus, be a good boy!" she said as she squeezed the little boy. "Thank you so much for everything," she tried to say through her tears.

"Let's go, Hannah," said the master.

When he had deposited her at the inn in Norfolk an

hour later, he gave her a small purse. She began to object, but he said firmly, "Hannah, this is yours. It is the wages you have earned during the past four years. You see, my dear, you never were a servant. You have always been a member of the family. We all love you. Have a happy life. Keep in touch, Hannah." With that he kissed her cheek, and was gone.

Part 4

Norfolk

Chapter 20

annah awoke to the pealing of church bells. At first she was totally disoriented. She placed her hand over her mouth to keep from shouting aloud, "Where am I?" Slowly, as always for her, it all came back. Her heart began to pound against her ribs in time with the pealing bells. She hadn't even realized that today was Sunday. She must get dressed and find someone who could direct her to the little church where she was to meet Will. Perhaps even now . . .

She dressed hurriedly, but with great care. Searching her memory, she remembered Will had often told her how beautiful she looked in blue, so she chose the deep blue dress Mistress Woodcutter had given her as a leave-taking gift. She carefully rebraided her hair, then wrapped the braids round and round in a crown on top her head. Giving herself one final glance in the glass, she pinched her cheeks for some color and set off down the hallway.

As she passed the desk, the innkeeper called out to her.

"Good mornin' to ye, Missy. The dining room is just openin'. Yer out early this fine day. I think the cook has coffee ready and can make you some flapjacks or—"

Hannah interrupted him. Though her stomach had already moaned to her several times this morning, eating was the farthest thing from her mind.

"Thank you, no," she replied anxiously. "You see, I must go to church. Can you tell me how to get to it? I hear its bells but . . ."

"Oh, so that's it. Well, ye'll probably be able to follow the call of the bells—but, it is nearly time for the service. 'Tis nigh onto a mile. Follow this street up six—no seven— blocks and then head west about a block and a half."

"Thank you," she called over her shoulder, already running out the door.

As Hannah raced to follow the sketchy directions the man had given, she tried mentally to prepare herself for the fact that Will probably would not be at the church yet today. But what her mind knew to be fact, her heart was not ready to accept.

Her mind raced ahead of her so much that she did not even glance at her surroundings. She'd paid no attention when Mister Mark had brought her to town yesterday as to where the inn was. Now her feet raced through a section that Norfolkians referred to as Uptown. There were several stores, some general, while others specialized in particular items. Each had signs on the windows advertising special prices, but Hannah did not even glance at them as she raced to the church.

"Remember," she told herself, "Captain Phillip said he was sold to a man hundreds of miles to the south of here. So, even if he was released yesterday as I was, there is no chance he's going to be here." But then her heart took over the argument. "Mayhap he could have been released early. He might be there searching for me."

Just as she rounded the corner and the church came into view, the bell stopped tolling, signaling that the service was to begin. Hannah had slowed to a dejected walk. For when she saw the church, she had immediately realized that it was not the right one.

In the four years since the *Wedgewood* had landed, the town of Norfolk had nearly doubled in size. In deep despair Hannah realized that she had no idea of how to find the meeting place she and Will had settled upon so hurriedly four long years ago. She gazed across the skyline, but she was in an area of two-story homes and could not see any church spires except the one in the next block.

Head hanging low, she walked along muttering to herself. "If my fondest hopes are true, and he is there waiting on me, he will think that I am not coming." Tears just below the surface threatened to rise. Just then she heard a strange voice.

"Hey lady—how 'bout a cabby to take you where'ere you're goin' today?"

A man had pulled up beside her in a small surrey pulled by a tired-looking old mare. Hannah's face must have registered shock, for she never dreamed that Norfolk had grown to the point that cab service would be either necessary or available. The many years of needing to count every penny she spent were not easily forgotten.

"Oh no—I couldn't . . ." she began, but then stopped. She did have the money which Mister Mark had paid her. Perhaps this cabby was an answer to a prayer she had not even prayed yet. He might be able to guide her to the place she sought. He was an elderly man and seemed safe. Hannah said, "Wait! Mayhap I *could* hire your services today."

She was helped into the surrey by the kindly old gentleman.

"Where to, lady?" he asked.

"Sir, I don't really know."

He stared at her as if she'd gone daft. "I can't take you till I know where it is you want—"

"I know. Please just listen for a minute." Embarrassment and frustration brought the unbidden tears to her eyes. "Sir," she stammered, "four years ago I came to this city by ship. Near the place where we came ashore there was a . . . well, it was a . . . chapel, or a church of some sort. I don't know—I don't even know the name of the church. But I know it was pretty—and it had a steeple. Can you—do you know—"

The old man interrupted her. "You just sit back and relax, little missy. I think I know exactly where you mean. The only church building I know of that is close to the water front is St. Luke's Episcopal. I'll have you there is just a few minutes."

Hannah closed her eyes and leaned her head back, but relaxation just would not come. Her heart began to race again. Maybe, just maybe, her beloved Will would be waiting for her! She sat up and tried to watch the way they traveled thinking to retrace these roads to get back to the Inn.

"Is that the place you want, lady?"

Hannah saw the harbor to her left. She followed the cabby's bony finger with her eyes. And yes, just across from it was the awful stump where she and Will had been so humiliated. There it was!

"Yes! Yes!" she shouted, unable to keep the excitement from her voice. Opening her reticule, she asked, "How much do I owe you?" She settled the debt, and descended from the surrey, racing the few steps to the church.

She pulled open the door, and found herself face to face with an elderly black gentleman.

"Can't let you in lady. Services done already begun, long time ago!"

"Oh please—I won't bother anyone. I have to get in and—"

"I's the sexton here, Ma'am. And I says who gets in and

out! Vicar Martindale, he don' wan' no 'sturbances to de services—specially near to de end, like dis. Now, you come on time next week, lady!" With that he pulled the door closed.

Hannah's frustration grew. She was so discouraged that she leaned her head against the door and finally let the tears flow. She did not know how long she stood thus, but before her tears of exhaustion and frustration were spent, the door reopened and the congregation began to file by.

Hannah began to hope again as she shrank back into the shadow of a nearby tree. Maybe her Will would come out and she could surprise him. She searched each face until all had come past her vantage point, but she recognized none of them. Just as she was about to turn away, she heard a familiar voice.

"Why, thank you for caring, Vicar," a well-dressed lady said as she shook the Reverend's hand. "Little Walter is nigh fully recovered from his bout with the mumps. We left him home with our neighbor this morning. It was good for me to get out and back to the house of the Lord. I enjoyed your serm— Oh my! Can it be? Is that you, little Hannah?"

"Miz Planter!" Hannah whispered, tears again streaming down her face. She had not realized how lonely she was for something—someone—familiar. The two ladies stood embracing and laughing and crying all at once.

Cookie interrupted them. "That's Mrs. Michaels, if you remember!" Hannah was shaking his hand as he answered his wife. "Yes, dear, I remember little Hannah from the ship. What are you doing . . . but, come! Take your noonday meal with us and we can get caught up on each other's lives."

While they talked, he had also herded them toward a small carriage. Soon they were heading down the street, with both ladies talking at the same time. Hannah had never been happier to see anyone in her entire life. She even forgot, for a moment, her disappointment that this was not to be the day she would be reunited with her Will.

* * * * * * * * * * *

Will wondered for the hundredth time that day how far he had walked and how much farther it could be to Norfolk and his beloved Hannah. He tried to keep his mind focused on seeing her again. Sometimes a hint of doubt would surface. After all, it had been more than four years since their separation. Mayhap she had found someone . . . but no! Not his Hannah! "She will be there waiting for me. I must hurry," he kept repeating to himself.

He followed a crude map which had been given him when he stopped for water by the humble home of his old acquaintance, Hank. Hank had reminded him of some of the major landmarks he would come to, and informed him of some new things to look for which had been built during his servitude. Hank had felt bad not being able to help him in his trek northward.

"I can hardly believe ye lived through that four years under da Demon. I'd give anythin' to be able to lend ye a mount or give ye a ride—but in truth, man, ye've caught me at the worst possible moment. I hafta haul this load of apples to da cider press in Meyersville today or lose da whole load. And da apples was the only crop which did anythin' for me this year. Fact is, Stivers, I gotta leave right now or I'll not make da press afore the line is too long to wait. God speed, my man. I hope ye find all yer lookin' for in Norfolk."

Will still smiled, even after two full days, when he remembered how Hank had driven the mule out of the yard. Will doubted the wagon would make it the three hour trip southward to Meyersville anyway—and if *it* did, the mule might not.

Thus far, Will had been given rides twice on his journey, in farm wagons. But in each case he had caught the folk just before they had needed to turn off his route. So in actuality, he had only ridden about ten miles total. He was trying to pace himself, knowing if he weren't careful, he risked another bout with the dreaded malaria. But the longing for Hannah pushed him forward and dulled his concern for his own safety.

Thus he pressed ever onward, and just now he was admiring the beauty of God's creation. The road Hank had mapped for him led across the top of a low range of mountains. He followed the ruts of wagons, wondering why anyone would choose to drive this path when down in the valley there surely was an easier route. To his left, the mountain rose sharply. And to his right, it was nearly straight down. Just ahead, he could hear a waterfall. A spring shot out of the rock just below the road. Will found himself at the top of the falls. Just as he arrived, the sun hit the falls in such a way as to throw hundreds of rainbows in every direction. Will knelt at the edge of the road and held his tin cup to taste of the spring.

He never knew exactly why it happened. Mayhap the rumble of the waterfall had blotted out his hearing. Mayhap the beauty of the place had him mesmerized. In any case, he looked up and was startled to see a wagon coming right for him at breakneck speed. All he could see were the pounding hooves of the four horses.

Without thinking of the consequences, acting on instinct alone, he dove over the edge of the cliff. He remembered clutching frantically for twigs, a rock, anything. Then there was an explosion of pain in the calf of his left leg as it struck something. Though he struggled valiantly to stay alert, and fight the pain, Will saw the jagged edge of the bone protruding through his lower leg, and a total darkness, which almost seemed a blessing, overcame him.

"What hap—where am I?" Will muttered, struggling to sit up. He was in a farm wagon, being jostled ferociously as the horses sped over the trail. Every bounce and bump sent blinding pain through his leg.

"Hey!" he tried to shout, but was so weak his cry was no more than a whisper. Trying to ignore the awful pain, he ushered all his strength to attract the driver. "Help!" he bellowed.

"Oh, so yer awake now—eh?" the big red-faced man said, as he reined in the horses. "Well—alls I know I kin say is that I am sorry, man. I never saw ye there at the top of Willow Spring Falls until ye were a-flyin' through the air."

Vaguely Will began to remember his dive to avoid a wagon . . . and horses . . . *these* very horses. "Where are we? How did you . . .?" he muttered. But every word was an effort. He fell back against the hay, wringing wet with sweat. His left leg felt as if it was afire.

The driver never left the seat of the buckboard. "I crawled down that cliff and carried ye back up to the road. Yer leg is all busted up. 'Tis thankful ye should be that ya passed out earlier. I'm a drivin' ya—several miles outen my way, I might add—to the doctor. Hopin' he can save that leg of your'n. Sorry if the bumpin' around bothers ya but from the amount of bleedin' that leg's a-doin' I think we better hurry. I bound it tight as I could in my old coat. We'd better git goin'." He turned as if to whip the horses.

"Please," Will interrupted. "Water! Can I?"

The big sun-burned man tossed him a canteen and watched as he drank.

"How long?" Will whispered, for the sun was hidden in an overcast sky. He had no idea how long he had been unconscious.

167

"Couple hours. Three maybe. Won't be long now till I get ya to Doc Hatfield's! Bite your tongue, man. It's gonna hurt again. Giddap!"

As the driver cracked the horses again, the jostling sent wave after wave of nauseating pain along Will's leg. He tried to raise on his elbow enough to see the leg, but could not fight the oblivion that came as he again lost consciousness.

When next he awoke he was between fresh clean sheets, in the softest featherbed he could remember since leaving the castle. The sun was shining through spotless windows which were outlined with crisp white princess-style curtains. As he struggled to sit up, a vision of utter loveliness entered the doorway. *An angel*, he thought, in his muddled state.

The angel spoke. "Best lie still, Mr. Stivers. It'll take you a while longer to build up strength. 'Tis a mighty sick man you have been. Poppa thinks atop of the fever caused by the poison in your broken leg, you maybe had malaria."

It was no angel but a girl speaking to him. No more than a child, really, twelve or thirteen years at the most. Her hair was the exact shade of sorrel red that his favorite horse had been back in Germany. It hung in natural ringlets and circles almost to her waist. Her eyes were the color of emeralds. Underneath a starched white pinafore she wore a simple navy blue dress. Atop the red curls perched a jaunty little white hat, one like the nurses in hospitals back in the old country wore. She was carrying a bowl of steaming chicken broth, which she deftly began to feed Will before he could protest.

"How long have I been here, Missy?" he asked between sips of the delicious broth.

"Let's see—'twill be three weeks tomorrow, Mr. Stivers," she replied.

"How do you know my name? I don't remember anything about . . ." he mumbled.

168

"Poppa found your manumission papers in your hat after that horrid old Mr. Parkerson brought you here."

"Parkerson?" Will questioned.

"He's a big crude oaf who lives over the mountain. Said he nearly hit you with his wagon. He just dumped you here for Poppa to fix and drove off."

"Now I remember," Will responded. "But if that was three weeks ago, what has happened to me since?"

A deep voice responded from the doorway. "Well, sir, I set your leg. 'Twas broke in two places, you know. And between Elly and me, we have been changing plasters and poultices every twelve hours since then till a few days ago, a-drawing the poison out of that leg. But you were outta your head with fever and chills and all. Are you susceptible to malaria, Mr. Stivers?"

It had been a long speech. Will had sized up Dr. Hatfield as he spoke and instantly liked the man. His daughter bore his red hair and green eyes. The man seemed knowledgeable, but more than that, kindly also.

"Yes, I've had several bouts with malaria. I—uh—I don't know what to say. I must have been an awful chore to care for. I apologize. I don't have any money. I—oooh!" As he had tried to move, he felt the awful aching in his leg.

"Eleanor, you leave Mr. Stivers and me alone now."

"Yes, Poppa," said the lovely girl as she rose and went out, closing the door behind her.

"She's a fine little nurse," said the proud doctor, "but I thought you might like some privacy." Doctor Hatfield explained his wounds and the method of treatment he had used. He also showed him the healing incision with over fifty stitch marks still showing where he had used cat gut to hold the leg together. He removed and replaced a bandage, re-tightened a splint, and finally wiped Will off from the waist up with a cool cloth.

Lying back, exhausted from the ordeal, Will mumbled,

169

"How will I ever pay you?"

"Just by getting well, Mr. Stivers. When I chose to be a doctor, it was to help people—not to get rich! You'll be up and around and fine in a couple weeks."

"Oh, before that! I must be! I have to get to Norfolk! Someone waits! I must!" Will exploded.

"Steady, man—relax! I need to go to Norfolk myself for supplies. I plan to leave on the Wednesday, a week from tomorrow. Should put us there on Saturday. If you are strong enough, I'll take you. But that is a mighty big if, old man!"

"I'll be strong enough," Will muttered, falling asleep in contentment.

* * * * * * * * * * *

"Oh Hannah. Do not despair. He will come. You must keep believing in him and in the promise you made to each other on yon stump."

For the fourth week in a row, Hannah's eyes were moist as she climbed into the carriage after church.

The Michaels had graciously invited her to stay with them until Will came for her. In actuality, Hannah's arrival had been a godsend to them. For Miz Planter-Michaels (whom Hannah now knew as Drusilla) was about halfway through a troublesome pregnancy. Hannah had quickly fallen into her old role of governess to four-year-old Walter. And she served as Cookie's helper and lady-in-waiting to Drusilla. The arrangement worked out well for all concerned. Hannah had a home and friends to help her get through this awful period of waiting. And the Michaels family had found the trusted servant they needed without ever advertising.

The home of these dear friends seemed almost meager in its furnishings after the grand mansion Hannah had

170

lived in at the Woodcutterrs. The entire house here could have been placed inside the Woodcutter's drawing room! But it was a home full of love and darling displays of needlework, flowers cut from the tiny garden, and homey touches.

Hannah learned her way around in no time. It was a bungalow, long and low. One entered directly into a parlor, with a small bedroom to the left. Behind the parlor through a large open archway, was the dining room, a smaller bedroom off its left. And behind the dining room was a kitchen with another bedroom off its left. Hannah occupied the tiny rear bedroom. It had been painted a pale rose and when the morning sun hit it just so, Hannah said, "It glows!" Walter Wedgewood was still in a crib in the small middle room, and Cookie and Miz Planter-Michaels slept in the front.

"Drusilla, thank you for trying to cheer me, but the longer the time grows the more I am convinced that . . ." Her voice broke. She could not go on.

As Cookie reined in the horses at the mounting block, Hannah gained control of herself. She descended first, reaching up for Walter to jump into her arms from his seat next to his father. Then Hannah tenderly helped Drusilla out of the carriage.

"I must begin to plan for the rest of my life," Hannah confided that afternoon after placing Walter down for a nap.

"What do you mean?" Cookie and Drusilla responded in unison.

"I think I must face the reality that something has happened to Will. Captain Phil said he was hundreds of miles south of here—but even at that, if he was coming, he would have been here by now." Her voice broke, but she forced herself to continue. "It has been an entire month. I just—I just wish I knew what I should do now!"

Drusilla interrupted. "Hannah, don't lose hope. Mayhap he is only detained somewhere. You need not make any decisions just now, sweetheart! We need you desperately. Cookie will double your wages. Walter adores you and I—"

Now it was Hannah's turn to interrupt. "I don't want more money. I told you I would help here just for the room and board. But I just don't want to impose. I'm so confused."

Cookie and Drusilla insisted that she stay on and would not take no for an answer. Hannah helped Drusilla prepare little garments for the baby, and taught Walter his ABC's.

Every day when Walter napped she took a long walk along the shore of the bay. Every day she stood at the stump and stared at the church. Her prayers were varied in length and content, but each time, before she left the stump, she looked to the top of the church steeple and whispered, "Please God—let him come."

* * * * * * * * * * *

Will grew stronger with each passing day. Doctor Hatfield fashioned crutches, but his patient soon discarded them in favor of a cane. Eleanor's delicious dishes roused his appetite and gave him much-needed nourishment.

On his first venture outside he went to a wash basin on the porch. He splashed water on his face, but as he reached for the towel he let out a shriek!

"No! It can't be!"

"What is it, Mr. Stivers?" Eleanor asked, racing from the kitchen as she dried her hands on her apron.

Will was staring into the glass window. An old man stared back at him where his own face should have been. He suddenly realized that he had not seen himself in a mirror since departing the *Wedgewood*. He was horrified.

"Mr. Stivers," the girl repeated. "Are you alright?"

"Oh Missy, ye'll think me a fool indeed. I just cannot believe that that—" he gestured toward the glass, "that that is me!"

She laughed. "Come inside. You are a bit unkempt. I can help some."

Will allowed the young girl to lather and shave him, realizing he was still too weak to try it himself. Then she trimmed and combed his hair, chatting gaily all the while. Finally she stood back and smiled, nodding her head. Handing him a small mirror, she asked, "How's that?"

Will took a long look from all sides and shook his head. "Aye! 'Tis much better, Miss Eleanor. At least I don't look like a wild man now. But I did not know my hair was white. I look so—so old!"

"How old are you, Stivers?" the doctor asked as he entered the kitchen from his office in the front of the house.

"I'm 23—no, 24, if it is past the date of November the 12th. But I look—oh, I just can't believe this white hair."

Luckily Will had not seen Eleanor gasp for breath as he revealed his age. She would have guessed him closer to twice that number of years.

"Well, Mr. Stivers, malaria will oft take the color out of one's hair. Don't worry about it. You don't look old in the face," the doctor lied. "But from the scars on yer back, I'm thinking you have been through enough to age anyone!"

On Wednesday morning, Eleanor handed her father a well-stocked basket of food.

"Yes sir," she answered for a tenth time. "As soon as I milk of an evening, I will go down to stay at Missus Clayborn's for the night. Just you be careful. Don't forget the rose-colored wool for my new shawl. I will see you next week."

Will walked from his room, unaided.

"No cane?" the doctor asked. "Aren't you pushing it a bit?"

"I'm going to walk to my Hannah with no help," he replied.

The doctor and his daughter exchanged smiles. She said, "Just be careful. I don't want all my nursing to go to waste, Mr. Stivers."

After goodbyes and hugs all around, they were on their way. Will thought the trip would never end. His leg ached severely, but he was determined not to let on. The doctor kept a lively conversation going much of the time, but was careful to watch Will for signs of weariness. Each afternoon he forced his companion to nap on a mattress prepared for that purpose in the back of the wagon. Each evening, they stayed with friends of the Hatfields. So the trip was truly no more of a hardship on Will than staying on in the cottage would have been. He was bone-weary, but almost giddy with the knowledge that every mile took him nearer to Norfolk.

Late in the afternoon of the third day, the doctor reached back and shook Will awake.

"There it is, Stivers! Yonder lies Norfolk!"

Directly in front of the wagon stood St. Luke's Episcopal Church, her spire still pointing toward heaven. Realizing that it was Saturday, and that he had no knowledge of Hannah's whereabouts, he tried to relax as the horses headed on up the shoreline drive to the friends of Doctor Hatfield.

Will could not take his eyes off the brilliant white finger of faith. "Tomorrow," he whispered, wiping tears of happiness from his eyes.

Chapter 21

s had always been their custom, the Michaels family arrived for church the next day just a few minutes before services began. It had turned quite chilly during the night, so Hannah and Cookie each carried large heated stones wrapped in blankets. After Cookie had closed and latched the door to their pew, Hannah placed the heated stones on the floor. Drusilla placed her dainty feet on one of them. Hannah sat on the angled bench at the end of the pew, sharing her heated stone with Walter. He sat to the edge of the main pew so his feet would reach. As always, Hannah found it hard to concentrate on the service when sitting on the angled bench. Always her eyes were drawn to the windows across from her or to the rear of the sanctuary.

The organ had just finished the last note of the prelude when the door opened again. Hannah was glad that the crotchety old sexton had bent his rules to allow the old man entrance, for it was so cold and she saw the wind blowing briskly in the trees through the windows.

Something drew her to watch this old man as the sexton directed him to the pew designated for visitors, third from the back. He was stoop-shouldered, and dragged one leg at a funny angle, but his eyes—they were so dark and piercing. And he seemed to be looking for someone. He looked vaguely familiar, in some way Hannah could not grasp.

"No Walter, we do not whisper in church," Hannah corrected the little boy. 'Twas a trial indeed to keep this one quiet for the hour-long service each week. "Say your ABC's in your head till preaching is done and see how many times you can get through them," she whispered into his ear.

The old man was huddled over in the drafty old church when Hannah ventured another peek toward the rear of the sanctuary.

He seems so—where could I have ever seen him before? Hannah wondered under her breath. She valiantly tried to keep her mind on the service, but had to smile each time Walter raised another finger. He had repeated the alphabet ten times and now Hannah held up one gloved finger for him since he was out of counting devices.

A movement from the visitors' pew caught her attention. As Hannah stared, the old man drew his hands out of his pockets. He wore snow white mittens! Not the dark gloves which men of fashion wore today. They were just like the ones she had—.

Just then Will raised his eyes and some force of fate drew them to the Michaels' pew. As he stared directly at Hannah, Will's eyes were lit from a fire within.

Walter Wedgewood took another of Hannah's fingers and pulled it out straight, beginning again. He whispered, "A-B-C-D . . ."

Hannah did not even feel the child's fingers on hers. Suddenly she realized that the white mitten now lifted in a silent salute was the one she had knitted on a long ago journey to freedom. Tears of joy coursed down her cheeks and she trembled all over, but not from cold!

"Hannah, what is it?" whispered Drusilla, ignoring the glare from the vicar.

"He's here! My Will is here!" she whispered in reply. Only a valiant effort kept her from shouting the words.

As the organ began the notes of the postlude, nothing could have held Hannah in the Michaels' pew. Throwing all propriety to the wind, Hannah pushed through the crowd. People who normally would have been upset by the jostling and lack of decorum seemed to sense that something out of the ordinary was happening, and a path opened up between the lovers. Will struggled to his feet, holding on to the cane with both hands till he could grasp the pew. Hannah pushed her way into the pew in front of him. Their eyes never left each others' and both her blue ones and his black ones filled with tears.

"Oh My Lady," he choked. "I was so afraid you wouldn't be here.

"Oh Will," she whispered, as he reached over the pew, covering her mouth with his own.

Gasps were heard from all around. "In the house of the Lord?" someone condemned.

They broke apart then, Hannah suddenly blushing furiously as she remembered where they were.

"Where better for us to be reunited than in the house of the One who brought us together in the first place, kept us alive for each other for four years, and now brought us *back* together . . . forever?" Will asked the crowd. Even the most straight-laced of the congregation smiled.

Much had transpired in one week's time. In spite of his weakened back and leg, Will had already found a good-paying job at the glass works where the Witherspoon boys also worked. He had also rented a small bungalow for them to live in.

The house he'd rented was an exact replica of the one Hannah would leave behind at the Michaels. An enterprising Scotchman had built a long string of them just alike and rented them now to the non-landowners and newcomers to America. The only way to tell them apart was the color of the front door and shutters. Drusilla and Cookie's had been red. The Stivers', four blocks away, was purple. Each block had the same sequence of colors— black, red, green, blue, orange, purple, brown. From a distance Hannah thought the tract of "Scotty's Rented Homes" (as the area was beginning to be called) resembled little Marcus' building blocks. Those first weeks and months together were to be so happy that Hannah would not even mind the purple door and shutters, even though purple was the only color Hannah was not fond of.

While Will planned their future life, Hannah, Drusilla, and the vicar had planned their wedding. Word had been sent to the Woodcutter family and it so happened that even Captain Phillip was in port and could attend the ceremony. It would be a bitter pill for him to swallow, but even he would feel happiness as he saw the utter transparency of Hannah's deep joy.

Cookie escorted a radiant Hannah down the aisle of St. Luke's Church. At the end of the aisle, Will stood, glowing with pride in his beloved. She was wearing blue, his favorite color, and her hair hung loose around her shoulders, at his request. Even the sober-faced vicar allowed himself to smile, for happiness permeated the little sanctuary.

Her voice broke as Hannah repeated after the vicar the age-old words from the book of Ruth. "And where thou lodgest, I shall lodge. Thy people shall be my people, and thy God—my God!"

At the close of the ceremony a party was held in honor of Mr. and Mrs. William Stivers at the home of the

Michaels. Cookie had outdone himself with a three-tiered cake. When the guests had all eaten their fill, an informal sort of receiving line formed as they took their leave.

Louisa and Daniel Witherspoon still looked like honeymooners themselves. "Hannah," Louisa whispered, "I want you to be the first to know. There's to be a baby in the spring!" Hannah squeezed the girl. Each thought herself the happiest person on earth.

Next in line came Karla and Chad, carrying little Marta who had fallen asleep during the party. "Hannah, now I understand why you cried so at my wedding. Why did you never tell us of your own plans for the future? We were often so insensitive."

Hannah's mouth hung open in dismay. "How did you know I cried? Little Marcus couldn't even talk!"

"Samantha saw, and gloated over your sorrow. I could never understand it, and it has always bothered me!"

"'Tis in the past. And as to my silence, my hopes for a future with Will were so deep—so special—that I could talk of them with no one."

Chad pulled on Karla's arm. "Tis late."

The expressive Karla kissed Hannah, pulling Will into a three-way embrace. "You, be good to our Hannah, Mr. Stivers. You must be special else she wouldn't love you." Pulling back, she stared at him. "He looks old, Hannah—but he is handsome!"

They were off in a cloud of giggles.

Next in line came Mistress Woodcutter. She and Hannah clasped hands and stood speechless. Tears came to both of them before her old mistress finally spoke.

"'Twas a beautiful wedding, Hannah. It felt—holy. It felt like we were in the presence of God. You are a lovely bride. And you are a very lucky man, Mr. Stivers. Hannah is so special. I will always believe that she is responsible for saving my home from disaster. We love her, and so we love you, too!"

Will was deeply touched. He stared at his bride in amazement, realizing there was much for him to learn about her.

Mark, carrying little Marcus, came next. "Will you consider being our guests for Christmas dinner, Mr. and Mrs. Stivers?"

"We shall, kind sir!" Hannah joked. "We'll be there!" she called as they walked away.

Turning back, Hannah found herself face to face with Captain Woodcutter.

"Miss Hannah, for the first time I understand. I see that what I hoped could never have been. Yours is a very special love. Congratulations, Stivers! Ye are a very lucky man."

Will answered, "'Tis not luck, Captain. 'Tis the blessing of an Almighty God."

As the captain left, Will turned questioning eyes to Hannah. The mysteries about her seemed to grow by the minute.

"Later, dear. I'll explain," she said.

The newlyweds donned their cloaks and prepared to walk the few blocks to their waiting home. Hugs all around left Walter Wedgewood crying tears of frustration. "Where's Miss Hannah going?"

"I'll see you in a few days," Hannah called as Will pulled her down the sidewalk.

'Twas a cold clear night with a full moon reflecting on the water, and a star-studded sky.

"Are you up to a bit of a walk, my lady?" Will asked.

"I could dance all the way to heaven and back," she responded. "But what of your leg? Surely it is tired!"

"Aye—but there is something we must do. I've dreamed and hoped and planned it for four years."

They walked arm in arm right past the little bungalow

180

and on to the corner where they had passed the first milestone on their trip to freedom in America. They stood in front of the horrid old stump, wordlessly. Will drew Hannah into a tight embrace. "Hannah Stivers, I love you!" he said as he kissed her long and passionately.

Without words, they crossed to the little old St. Luke's Church. Their minds seemed to be woven together as one.

Will knelt on his right knee, keeping his stiff bad leg out at his side. Hannah knelt beside him on the steps. But instead of bowing their heads, they both looked straight up to the top of the steeple.

"My Father—no, *our* Father" Will stammered. "Oh, what can I say except—thank You!"

"Amen!" Hannah added fervently.

Hannah shivered in the cold as they hurried toward their home, as fast as Will's limp would allow.

"Here, my lady," Will mumbled. "I can warm my hands in my pockets." And reverently he handed her the white mittens. Gratefully, she put them on.

* * * * * * * * * * *

Christmas morning dawned cold but sunny. There was just a trace of snow. Will had borrowed a buggy from the glass works. The tired old horse made the hour-long trip to the Woodcutters into a two-hour trip, but the Stivers did not care. They had so much to learn of each other and what had transpired during their four years apart that they never seemed to tire of talking.

Hannah had cried when she first saw Will's back. But her admiration and love for him grew as she learned it was due to his high standard of obedience to God's ancient command of keeping a holy Sabbath.

Will had marveled at the fact that though she had been offered the hand of the famous Captain Phillip Woodcutter, she had chosen to wait for him instead. It seemed that with each shared remembrance, their love for each other deepened.

The day at the Woodcutter house was special in so many ways. Little Marcus was almost angelic, entranced as he was with all the new toys. Baby Marta allowed Hannah to rock her to sleep, which was a treat for one who prayed daily for God to give her Will's child. Louisa announced to the entire family that a baby would come in the spring.

"If it's a boy, it shall be Daniel Junior. And if it is a girl, her name shall be Hannah!" Louisa added shyly.

Hannah dropped her head and tears of happiness flowed freely.

"Whilst she is crying anyway, I have an announcement to make," said Mister Mark, amid embarrassed laughter. "Or better stated—a proposition, I think." He cleared his throat meaningfully, then continued. "My sons-in-law have overheard Will here sharing his dreams and hopes for the future with some men at work. It seems he isn't very happy in the factory!"

"Aye, 'tis no secret!" Will responded. "I only took the job to be able to support Hannah and myself. I hope to be able to save the money to buy a farm someday. It's always been our dream—ever since Germany—to be free and farming our own land. Right, My Lady?"

Hannah nodded, having gained control of her tears. She stared at her old boss wondering what was to come next.

"Well, Will, as my wife so aptly stated on the night of your wedding, we owe our happiness as a family to your wife. Four years ago today we came close to losing all we have—if Hannah had not been there, I don't know what would have happened. Out of gratitude to her, and as our Christmas gift, we give you this."

He handed a slip of paper to them—a deed—for a fifty acre plot of ground adjacent to the Woodcutters' home.

He continued, "'Tis a useless strip of land to me. The timber has all been cut. And my wife wants neighbors—specifically, she wants Hannah! You can live here with us whilst you build yourselves a home. What say ye, Stivers? Is it okay?"

Will and Hannah were speechless. It was all they'd ever hoped for and more. Four long years at Demonland had broken down Will's pride which might earlier have caused him to bristle at such an offer. He stood to his feet and extended his hand.

"Mister Mark, my wife and I gratefully accept your gift. And may God bless you. Merry Christmas, one and all."

Hannah smiled through renewed tears.

Epilogue

Two months had passed. The new home would soon be ready. The winter had been mild, allowing Will and Mark to build nearly constantly.

"Tell me again about the mittens, Uncle Will," little Marcus asked that evening.

And so Will had patiently begun the story of the gift of wool from Frau Hohenburger, concluding it with Hannah recognizing him at the church because of the mittens. "They have always been a symbol of freedom to me, little Marcus," Will explained. "Even when I was delirious with fever at the plantation where I stayed, it comforted me to hold the mittens. Somehow they seemed to say to me that one day I would be free and with Hannah again. Do you understand?"

Hannah awoke the next morning. She planned her day in her mind as usual. "Today, I will begin . . ." she mumbled.

'Twas noon when Will came into the nursery. Hannah's old room which the Woodcutters had insisted that the Stivers now occupy.

"Hannah, have you seen my mittens?" he asked.

Hannah turned away, fumbling in her knitting bag. "No dear, I don't know where they are. You can probably borrow a pair of Mark's gloves!"

Will was amazed at Hannah's calmness. "But, My Lady—surely I haven't lost them. Not after all these years!" He grew more and more frustrated.

Hannah turned to him, her face glowing pink. "Will, darling, listen to me. You have not lost them. You see, I have unraveled them." She held up two balls of white yarn.

"But Hannah! How could you? I would have bought you yarn if you needed it! I—my—oh Hannah, why?" he asked with a note of despair in his voice.

"Please Will, let me explain. Don't grow angry. Just as the mittens had a special significance to you, they did for me—one I want to share with the next generation of Stivers."

"Of course we will tell them," Will replied exasperatedly. "We'll always remind our children of our long quest for freedom—what it cost us—how dear it is. But we could have shown them the mittens. I still cannot understand . . ."

"Darling, Will," she laughed. "Don't you see? Let me put it another way! What do you think of the name Freedom Stivers for a boy, or maybe Liberty Stivers for a girl? We could call her Libby! You see, in about six more months, another Stivers shall wear your white woolen mittens. The reason I unraveled them is so that I could begin to knit a baby's sweater with the yarn!"

"Oh, My Lady!" he sighed.